PERFIDIOUS

P. T. MCKENZIE

🏵 Created with Vellum

To Zac
Beloved and Never Forgotten

1250 – 1350 AD

Monsters once roamed the Earth, doing as they pleased, and humans feared the prowling beasts.

But in 1257, a knight decided he would conquer one such monster, a dragon. He cornered the dragon while it was sleeping and pierced it through the heart, hence by killing the monster. His actions taught the humans it was possible to fight against the creatures that hunted them.

By 1311, the number of monsters had dwindled at the hands of man. A human king named Scholet offered rewards of gold and jewels, encouraging the killing of multitudes of remaining monsters. His movement caused the monsters to hide within the world of man. Many creatures—dragons, gargoyles, shapeshifters, elves, fairies—learned how to appear human to escape being hunted.

But not all monsters were content with such an existence. In 1348, a once wild dragon known as Pierce rejected the falsehood to appear human. He rallied a variety of monsters to attack a human village known for housing numerous hunters. Many died on both sides. That battle, known as Pierce's Battle, was the first of many.

The Human Wars officially began on December 30th, 1348.

An excerpt from The King's Legacy:
A Complete History of Perfidious

1

As I stepped out of my bedroom window onto the dew-covered grass, I zipped up my sweater against the cool morning air. My head still felt groggy from crying myself to sleep the night before, but I faced the vast forest surrounding my house and headed down the familiar dirt path to the gate of Perfidious.

Being half-elf allowed me to see better than most humans, even with the pre-dawn woods being so dark. I walked under two maple trees whose branches entwined to form an arch—the southeastern gate of Perfidious. Being within its boundaries felt different compared to being outside of the gates. It was probably a placebo effect, but I felt more at home, like I could be myself. At first glance, there really wasn't a difference—same trees, same plants, same air. But the villages with pureblood monsters and half-breeds that existed further inside made Perfidious special.

The residents of Perfidious had established six main

villages for half-breeds, some located in the flatlands to the east, others in the forest nearby. I half jogged toward my second home on the outskirts of one of those forest villages, Coalfell. Birds chirped above in welcome. Without the sun, the cold clung to my skin, but I powered through, determined to finish my mission before school.

I smiled, reaching a familiar tall oak. During one of my first expeditions into Perfidious, I had found the old tree five minutes outside of Coalfell. The roots grew too large and spread out for much to survive near it, so it stood alone. An opening underneath had been almost large enough for me to walk around in, so I dug a little deeper and reinforced with dirt and wood to make walls and a ceiling. I added a trap door at the base of the tree, turning it into a hideaway that only few knew about. If someone passed by, they wouldn't even notice my little root cellar beneath.

I scanned my surroundings to make sure no one was watching before opening the door and jumping down into the darkness. A twin bed sat against one wall with my dresser a couple of feet away. In the bottom drawer, I had everything I wanted to keep hidden from my parents, including a small box. I grabbed a wire with a glow-in-the-dark star attached from the dozen in the box and made my way out of my hideout, back into the early morning light.

As I walked, I kept an eye out for anything that moved. Even though I was near a half-breed village, I still wasn't safe from the creatures that stalked the shadows. Few monsters wanted to venture into Coalfell due to its close proximity to humans, making it the safest place for half-breeds. However, it was safer to be on guard than be something's breakfast.

The forest was quiet except for the occasional breeze through the leaves. My eyes scanned the underbrush for signs of movement.

A shadow darted through the trees in front of me.

I bolted, running opposite of the creature, veering from the path as quickly as my legs would carry me. Footsteps crushed leaves behind me as I ran.

It was gaining on me.

Rays of sun bloomed in front of me from the clearing ahead. I hurried to it, whipping around in the open to confront the thing in pursuit. In a fighting stance, I scanned the area, looking for something I could use as a weapon, but it was too late.

Hand to hand combat it was. I raised my fists as a shadow approached the edge of the trees. A boy with black hair and fiery eyes slowly stepped into the sunlight.

My adrenaline dropped.

"Kalvin!" My heart raced, and I put my hands on my knees, trying not to melt from relief.

"Hey Elisia. Did I scare you or something?" His amused grin made me want to punch him.

"No, you didn't," I said, a little winded from the run. "What are you doing out here anyway? You're not exactly a morning person."

He snorted. "That's the truth. I'm on my way to my mom's. I saw you and figured ya'd want company?"

"Sure. I'm just heading to the Mourning Willow." I started walking back to the path.

Kalvin followed me, making almost no noise. We walked in silence, but I couldn't help looking over at him. His black hair hung just above his golden-orange eyes. Kalvin was an amazing fighter, extremely muscular—not the kind that looked weird, but enough that you could tell he'd win a fight.

Kalvin smirked as he glanced at me. "You like what you see?"

Heat rose to my cheeks, and I punched him. "Shut up."

He snickered but didn't say anything else. Kalvin always made flirty comments to me and every other girl, but it wasn't like he was serious. Someone watching us might think that we were dating or something, but even with all his talk, we'd only ever been just best friends. Nothing more.

We approached the willow in a small clearing at the end of the path. I ducked under its droopy branches and into the hidden beauty underneath. The Elders had turned the willow into a memorial for the half-breeds killed by purebloods within Perfidious, calling it the Mourning Willow. Hundreds of little trinkets hung from the branches, most of which had names on them for the half-breed they represented. I searched and found a bundle of new ornaments with "Dylan" on them. Reaching for the wired star in my back pocket, I threw myself up and fastened it around a thin branch.

Since the age of ten, I had hung a star for every half-breed who died in Coalfell, even if I didn't know them. And I didn't know Dylan very well, but I still honored his life, knowing his death would never find justice.

After making sure my star was secure, I turned back to Kalvin. His back was to me, his Anchor peeking out from his cut-off shirt.

Every half-breed has a mark on their left shoulder called an Anchor that almost looks like a tattoo but with a defining shimmer. No one knows why we have them. Some rumors claim they are brands caused by the mix of human and monster blood, marking us as less than purebloods. Kalvin's Anchor always reminded me of a fireplace, the bottom line only going halfway across and a squiggly line darting through the center of the box like a little flame.

"You're not taking a bag. Does that mean you're coming back tonight?" I jumped down from the tree.

"Yup." He turned to face me. "My mom didn't want me coming at all, not since Dylan..." Kalvin stopped and cleared his throat. "Anyway, she has something I need. I should be done by the time you get out of that human school. Wanna spar later?"

"Sure. We can meet at my root cellar. What does she have?"

He winked. "It's a secret. You'll find out later."

Kalvin walked me back to the edge of the forest by my house before he headed to the west side of Perfidious. Though the half-breeds stayed on the east side of Perfidious, most of our pureblood parents lived on the west side near the mountains. However, visiting was dangerous; many purebloods would not hesitate to kill a half-breed.

Whenever I heard news of one of us being murdered, it scared me. I couldn't imagine losing Kalvin, the only person I could talk to about both my elf and human problems. Few humans knew about Perfidious, so it's not like I could tell anyone at school.

I don't know what I would do without him.

I entered the light blue house through my bedroom window, hoping I could make it to school without getting yelled at for sneaking out. However, before I swung my second leg over the windowsill, my father opened the door. He leaned against the door frame, arms crossed, and stared at me with his bright blue eyes, the same color as mine.

"It's not what you think," I told him. I didn't want him thinking I stayed in Perfidious all night. They would ground me for sure. "I left early this morning."

"Why were you there this time?" he asked with a flat voice.

"I wanted fresh air."

His eyes squeezed shut as he touched his temple. The thing about my dad is that he has a rare elf ability that I sadly didn't inherit—he can tell when people are lying.

He took a minute before he looked at me. "Why don't you just tell me the truth? I will even make it easy for you. If you tell me, I won't tell your mother."

My lips thinned. She would not be happy if he told her. Mom didn't like it when I left the house without telling her.

I groaned. "I was at the Mourning Willow."

"Why?" A hard smile spread across his lips as though he found it funny. He raised his voice. "You didn't know him."

I bit my tongue. I couldn't say what I wanted. We didn't agree on anything to do with Perfidious or half-breeds.

We never would.

I pushed myself off the windowsill and stood firmly in front of him. He didn't want the truth, but his elf abilities make it impossible to just tell him what he wanted.

"Does it matter? We have this conversation every time I go there. Can't you just accept that I'm gonna go there, and

6

you can't stop me?" I realized too late that I said the wrong thing. He exhaled sharply and I spoke fast. "Ugh. That's not what I meant. I mean that going to the Mourning Willow isn't that bad. I could be doing way worse than hanging a star on a tree. But I'm not."

He took a step and opened his mouth to speak but stopped. He stood there in what seemed like a mental battle. I waited to see which side would win.

Finally, his shoulders relaxed a tad. "Were you alone?"

"No, Kalvin was with me."

My father took a deep breath, and his shoulders relaxed fully. "I guess as long as you weren't alone, then it could have been worse. But this doesn't mean I approve. You are part of my bloodline, Elisia. So, if you get into trouble in Perfidious or are spotted somewhere you shouldn't be, it would look bad for me. I have an important job at the castle, and it took me a long time to get it. Things you do could jeopardize my reputation. My position keeps you safe. You know this. But if you continue going to places like that willow, it won't look good on my part."

"Okay…" I was a half-breed and had every right to be at the Mourning Willow. But instead of telling him that, I chose a safer approach. "I'll try to stay out of trouble."

"I guess that's better than nothing."

I nodded and walked past him towards the kitchen where Mom was busy cooking breakfast. I snuck up behind her and used my inhuman speed to snatch a piece of sausage, which she might not have noticed if I wasn't playing hot potato with it.

Mom turned around. "It would've cooled down if you waited for me to take it off the burner."

I smiled at her. "I just couldn't help myself." I stuck the

stolen sausage into my mouth. "Plus, I have to get to school. I'm gonna be late."

I walked into the foyer to put my shoes on.

"Well, if you'd gotten home from your morning excursion earlier," she called after me, "then you wouldn't be rushing out the door."

I stopped what I was doing to gape at her. She didn't even look up—just focused on the food on the stove. I turned to my father and scrunched my nose, narrowing my eyes at him.

He held up his hands in surrender. "It wasn't me."

Mom failed to hold back a smirk. "I checked to see if you were up, but I found an empty bed and an open window. I put two and two together."

"Oh..." I looked down. "Well, I'm gonna go to school. Am I in trouble?"

"We'll see," my mom said, dropping the subject as she grabbed two plates.

I hugged her to gain some brownie points before I grabbed my backpack and left for school.

On the way, I put my chestnut hair up into a ponytail. I'm thankful I inherited most of my physical traits from my mom. Only the unnatural highlights and bright blue eyes made me look slightly inhuman. Though, sometimes I wished I had pointy ears like my dad. They would have annoyed me, but at least then I wouldn't have to go to a stupid human school.

Perfidious didn't exactly have anything that would compare to school. I'd take individual lessons from specialists in Coalfell with the other half-breeds. That would have been way more interesting than the classes the counselor told me I had to take.

I just hoped I wouldn't be late. That would draw too much attention, and attention for a half-breed is never a good thing.

2

I walked into school and made my way to my locker, sliding past dozens of people crowding the long hall. Every locker appeared the same—yellow and worn. The gold numbers "156" marked my locker, which creaked open as I put my backpack in and pulled my math books out. I looked at the clock hanging down the hall. My heart skipped a beat.

The bell rang.

Crap.

I jogged my way over to class. I hated being late, especially to math. Mrs. Walker always made a comment about tardy students. I quietly opened the back door to the classroom, hoping I could sneak in without getting busted.

"Ah. Thank you for joining us, Ms. Meyer," Mrs. Walker announced in front of the class. "Tardiness may cause dire consequences someday. Best to break that habit now." She pushed her glasses up, glaring at me.

I forced a smile and hurried to my seat in the back row. Although it comprised the older, squeaky desks that no one liked, I found it more alluring. I had the advantage of being on the outside, having everyone else in front of me, viewing everything going on without being in the middle. It meant, of course, that no one usually bothered me.

But that time, a guy sat in the normally empty desk next to my seat. I hesitated. His head was down, his light brown hair covering his face, but I knew who he was by his varsity jacket. He looked up, his moss green eyes meeting mine.

I sat down in my seat. "What are you doing back here, Greyson?" I whispered, trying to make it sound like I was joking instead of what I actually was—appalled. "Shouldn't the quarterback of our football team sit near the front with the other jocks?"

"Just thought I'd sit back here today. I wanted to see why you insist on sitting in the back row every class."

His explanation made little sense, but I tried to ignore it as I got my math book out. Greyson was a brilliant guy. But even though we had two classes together and had been in the same school since the 4th grade, we never really talked. The stereotypical quarterback of the football team, one of the popular kids, he was on the top, and I wasn't exactly fond of being noticed. Everyone's eyes were on the popular kids, and I didn't like that much attention from humans.

I looked over at Greyson. He was looking at me, but as soon as our eyes met, he looked away. Did he need something? He was acting strange.

I kept expecting him to try to talk to me during class, but he sat quietly until the bell rang. I didn't notice him much throughout the rest of the day, so I dismissed it.

My schedule ended with gym, my favorite because I

got to play sports I never would have otherwise. I rushed into the girls' locker room to change. Though I loved the class, it presented its own unique challenges for a half-breed—my Anchor.

I took my shirt off, and an excited gasp echoed behind me.

I groaned inwardly as I turned to see a shorter girl with blonde hair in perfect ringlets, her eyes glued to my shoulder.

"I love your tattoo! I don't think I've seen ink like that before. Where'd you get it?" The girl bounced slightly as she spoke, but talking about my Anchor made me nervous.

"I got it somewhere south a while ago. I don't remember the place," I lied, giving her my best fake smile.

Her excitement vanished, and she left me alone to finish getting ready for gym.

The little mark I was born with drew so much attention from humans. The slight shimmer made Anchors different from regular tattoos. Mine looked as though it was a crescent moon within a perfect circle. It wasn't anything special, but people always asked me where I got it. And I always had to lie.

I finished getting ready and jogged out to the gym. We had been playing floor hockey for two weeks, and I was the only girl on a team with five guys: three football players, Noah, Anthony, and Greyson; and two other boys, Ryan and Kyle.

Greyson and I always managed to break through the opposing team's defense for the score. His speed almost matched mine, which always made me curious. With me being half-elf, I would easily win in a race at top speed, yet it puzzled me how fast he was able to run for a human.

"Great pass, Elisia," Greyson complimented me after the winning goal, right before the bell rang.

"Thanks, Greyson. You too," I replied, turning to head to the locker room. I wanted to go back to Perfidious as soon as—

"Hey, Elisia."

I faced Greyson with an eyebrow arched and my sweat-soaked shirt clinging to my sides.

He avoided making eye contact as he scratched the back of his head. "There's a pool party at my house on Thursday. Noah's idea. It's supposed to be around...ninety? I think." He glanced at me with a half-grin.

"That's not really news. Noah has a new party brewing every couple of weeks." It confused me why he was telling me.

"I don't know if it'd be your kind of crowd, but would you maybe wanna come?"

I didn't answer. It wasn't like I got invited to any of the other parties he'd thrown. I blinked several times before he continued.

"Noah...He, um. He wanted me to ask you. He said we don't have to worry about homework because we won't have school on Friday." Greyson laughed nervously and shifted his weight.

"Um, maybe." I heard the uncertainty in my voice. "It sounds like fun. I'll just have to check if I can go."

Greyson's face brightened as he pulled a pen from his pocket. He reached out, grabbed my hand, and wrote something on my palm. "This is my number. Text me if you decide to come...or ya know, if you decide not to. Catch you later."

Greyson turned around and jogged to the boys' locker room.

I watched the way he went long after he was out of sight. I felt like I should have been wary. I looked down at the number on my hand. The handwriting was barely readable.

A gleam of excitement danced like butterflies in my stomach. I hadn't been invited to one of Noah's parties before. It wasn't like an invite was needed, but I still felt like I was too much of an outsider to go. Maybe I was over-thinking it. I shook my head, hoping it would quiet my thoughts and wrangle my mind back on track.

I needed to get to Perfidious.

In the girls' locker room, I copied the number into my phone and put my clothes into my gym bag. I ran out of the school and straight home, not wanting to miss my chance.

I was barely winded by the time I reached my house. For a human, running a mile in four minutes was an accomplishment. For me, running the mile and a half home from school in four minutes was easy at top speed. Being half-elf definitely had its perks.

My window was open, so I tossed my backpack and gym bag into my room as I passed it on my way into the woods.

Each time, Kalvin took the same route coming back from his mom's house—well, I guess it was more like a cave. I'd traveled with him a few times to visit her, but Kalvin usually went there on weekdays when I couldn't because of school.

Leaves crunched under my feet. I blazed through the gate and quickened my pace, hoping I'd make it in time.

The path he took was the one that led straight into the mountains. There was only one. I twisted and turned around the trees in my way.

Finally, the path was up ahead.

I jumped to the lowest branch of a tree that towered over the narrow dirt trail and started to climb. The branches swayed as I made my way into the canopy. Soft footsteps creaked in the distance. I slowly balanced my way to a space in the leaves and crouched. My hand tightened. The bark poked my skin.

Kalvin walked into view.

He almost appeared human. But I knew he wasn't, and I'd never underestimate him again.

It reminded me of when we first met. I was up in a tree very similar to that one. I had gotten a little lost and was trying to find any landmarks I recognized. Kalvin and his dad, Aaron, walked past the tree.

The boy, around the same age as me, noticed my bag and went to pick it up. I didn't want him to touch it. My seven-year-old self tried to pick a fight with him. He appeared human then, too, and I thought I could win the fight. After all, Dad had started teaching me the basics of how to throw a punch. I thought I was prepared.

But I didn't stand a chance.

This boy turned out to be half-dragon and was years ahead of me in training combat. After we settled down, Aaron helped me find my way home. Later, I stumbled upon them training and asked Aaron if he could teach me as well, since it seemed like my father had less and less free time away from his new job at the castle. He still wasn't home very often, and Aaron was dead.

I shook my head.

Focus.

Kalvin grew closer. I waited impatiently until he was directly underneath me.

I jumped.

My body cut through the air as my adrenaline pumped. I thought I would finally surprise him, but he looked up at the last second. His orange eyes narrowed as he sensed the present threat. Realizing it was me, his irises extended back into a circle, but his pupils still looked like dragon's eyes.

In a flash, he stepped to the side. His hands grasped my ankles mid-air and spun me around, sending me flying into a leaf pile. The leaves exploded around me.

That didn't go as planned.

I battled with the leaves to get them off. Kalvin laughed, which was contagious, and despite all my efforts, I smiled back at him. He extended his hand to me, but I simply stared at it. Close up, I could see the faint outline of scales on his skin.

After rolling my eyes, I accepted his help.

"I think ya almost got me?" Kalvin said as he gave me an encouraging shrug, but we both knew I wasn't even close.

I finally noticed the straps around his chest and the two swords strapped to his back. My frustration quietly faded.

My eyes widened. "Is one of those for me? Was this the secret something you had to get from your mom?" I asked, remembering he told me he would teach me how to fight with a real blade.

We usually worked with wooden staffs or wooden daggers, but that was only because I had never been interested in finding an actual weapon for myself. I just liked learning different hand-to-hand techniques. But ever since Kalvin started at his new job in Coalfell as an apprentice blacksmith, I'd been interested in trying something out. Kalvin suggested swords to start.

"Yup, Mom made'em for us. She made sure they're sharp, but not sharp enough to break my dragon skin. I'll still need to go easy on you, though," he said, unsheathing an elegant silver blade and handing it to me. "An elf's skin is not so tough."

"Ha! Wait 'til I learn how to use it. You'll be eating those words." I shifted my weight to my back foot, extending the sword towards him.

He raised his hands in fake surrender. "Sorry, Elisia. I know I said we'd spar, but I can't today. There's this village thing I forgot about. Argon is making me go. He said, 'an apprentice should be like a shadow.'" Kalvin rolled his eyes as he did an impression of what I assumed was supposed to be Argon, his boss. "Whatever that means. I was raised by a blacksmithing dragon, and he barely trusts me to sharpen a blade." He kicked a rock close to his foot.

I placed my hand on his shoulder. "I'm sure he'll let you do something soon. You've only been there for... what...a month?"

"Yup." Kalvin looked back at me, all doubt gone as his eyes met mine. "But trust me, I'd much rather be here to prove you wrong. Tomorrow?" He started backing away.

I nodded and bit my lip. "Alright...I guess I should probably head home too." My words made Kalvin stop in his tracks and sigh.

His shoulders slumped, and he tilted his head. "What'd ya do this time?"

I narrowed my eyes at him. "What makes you think I did anything?"

"I know you. Now spill." Kalvin still showed no emotion as he stared at me, an expression that always made me think he already knew what I was about to say.

"My parents caught me this morning. I may or may not be in trouble when I get back home."

Kalvin shook his head as a mischievous smirk appeared on his lips. "If you need to get away from your parents, my place is always available," he offered mischievously as he started walking backwards again.

"In your dreams," I responded, unfazed by his flirty comment. "Plus, I can't leave. I have to go to school."

"Oh right, that human nightmare you always complain about." Kalvin sounded mildly disappointed, but the smile remained on his lips.

"Yeah. Well, see you tomorrow, Kalvin." I waved as I ran off.

"Bye, Elisia! See you in my dreams."

1351 – 1450 AD

The monsters continued to fight back, but without a leader, their efforts were futile. Both sides of the Human War suffered loss after loss, and it appeared as though no side would be victorious. Blood stained the land.

King Scholet II discovered that neither side was prevailing. So, on March 4th, 1375, he posted a notice in every village stating his desire to convene with the leader of the monsters in hopes of discussing the terms of the war and a potential treaty.

No one came forth. Years passed, and new kings were born.

In 1406, a shapeshifter who had led many successful brigades against the humans appointed himself the leader of the monsters. He approached the human king, King Kloss, in human form while all the citizens expressed their concerns. Upon his turn to speak, the shifter stood before King Kloss and declared his true form, causing a raucous in the great hall. After much deliberation, King Kloss met with him to discuss peace.

The shapeshifter and King Kloss signed a treaty on June 9th, 1411 stating that there would be an area set aside for the monsters where humans would not hunt them. The shapeshifter was appointed king, and it was declared that should the land ever be without a central ruler, the treaty would become invalid.

They named the land Perfidious.

An excerpt from The King's Legacy:
A Complete History of Perfidious

3

I jumped through my open bedroom window and made my way to the kitchen, hanging my jacket on my door-knob. My stomach growled anxiously, so I opened the refrigerator and rummaged through its contents. Finding nothing, I closed the door to check the cabinet.

Unsure what to make, I paced around the empty house. Mom usually worked at the news station until seven. What would put Mom in a good mood? Maybe make dinner or clean up the house? I knew we'd be talking about me leaving without permission that morning. Buttering Mom up didn't always work, but it was worth a shot.

I got to work straightening up the house. It needed to be vacuumed, dusted, and mopped. Mom liked to make sure we always had ingredients for easy meals, so dinner was the easy part—spaghetti.

After dinner finished cooking and was set aside for serving, I paced the kitchen, listening for Mom's car. I checked the clock again. 7:06. She would be home at any moment. My heart jumped at every car that passed by our house.

Why was I so nervous?

It wasn't about sneaking out.

Greyson's party.

I'd never asked to go to a party before, but that's what normal kids did. Humans went to parties all the time and hung out with their friends. Maybe Mom would say yes.

A car slowed down near our driveway.

Headlights blinded my vision as I peeked out the window. Rushing back to the kitchen, I grabbed two bowls and dished out the spaghetti. My ears focused on the sound of her heels clicking up the walkway, the jangle of her keys in the lock, and finally the door opening and closing.

"Dinner's done," I called to her.

Mom shrugged off her coat, her tired eyes brightening as she made her way into the dining room. She grabbed a fork and dove in before I had a chance to set it all the way down.

"Sorry, hun," Mom said between mouthfuls. "Busy day…no time for lunch…needed food."

I laughed. "Did something interesting actually happen in this town?"

She nodded and slowed down eating. "I mean, it's not anything unusual. A reporter started looking into the disappearances around the forest line that leads to Perfidious. I had to find an even bigger story than his to deter him."

"Did you find anything?"

"Eh, some medical supplies went missing at the hospital. By the evidence, it looks like they were just misplaced, but he's new. He's trying to find stories where there are none. I placed enough doubt in his mind for him to dive into the investigation."

I nodded and the sound of chewing again filled the air. After it seemed like my mom had relaxed, I decided to ask her about the party, my sweaty hands fidgeting in my lap.

"So..." I elongated the word, trying to get her attention. "There's this party that I got invited to by a guy from school. It's the day after tomorrow. Can I go?"

Mom set her fork down. "Hm." She didn't say anything else for a few moments. It felt like hours as she sat there, her lips thin. Finally, Mom turned her gaze toward me. "There's a chance I'll let you go. But first, let's talk about how much trouble you're in after this morning."

I cringed. I was hoping she'd forgotten about that. "Right...This morning...I, um, I was only going to the Mourning Willow. I wanted to go before school. And if I waited until you were awake to ask you, I wouldn't have made it. And I wasn't alone. Kalvin was there. He walked with me."

Mom raised the corner of her lips. "I know. I talked to your dad. He seems to think you're spending too much time in Perfidious, and that you shouldn't have gone to the Mourning Willow."

"Is Dad still here, or did he already leave?" I already knew the answer.

"He already left." Mom paused before she spoke next. Her words seemed slow and calculated. "Your dad doesn't like to spend much time away from the castle. That's why he's only here once or twice within a week."

I stabbed my fork into the noodles with more force

than I needed. "It's not fair that he doesn't like me being in Perfidious, but he rarely leaves."

"Elisia, it's different for you." Mom sighed. "Being a half-breed, you're in a lot more danger in Perfidious. I know you and Kalvin are always together, but from what your father is telling me, you're not making smart decisions over there."

"Mom, I promise you. I've been training in combat since I was seven. I know how to protect myself."

Mom took my hands. "So, this party. Where is it?"

I struggled to find the words. "Um, down the road. Not far. I think it's about a mile or so?"

She nodded, but it seemed as though she was agreeing to something inside her own head. "You can go to the party."

My eyes widened. *She was letting me go?* I lost all brain function and didn't remember how to speak.

Mom's smile grew. "It's a chance for you to hang out with your classmates. I'm not going to say no to that. But you will have extra chores, including making dinners some nights." She took a bite of her spaghetti. "I think we both need more home cooked meals."

"Deal." It was the only word I could form. I couldn't believe she was letting me go. Wasn't I supposed to be in trouble? I expected a grounding or something a little more extreme.

Mom pointed her fork at me. "You're also cleaning up dinner. I'm way too tired, and I need a bath."

I nodded and went back to eating my food. After dinner, I took care of dishes per the agreement and made sure Mom had a container for leftovers. I had more homework, but I needed a chance to sit down before I did it. I laid my head down on the couch, grabbed the remote, and turned it to a show about people surviving in the wilderness. My eyes quickly got heavy. At some point, I dozed off.

Pain radiated through my body. I couldn't remember getting hurt. I limped forward. Two pathways stretched out before me. I knew I had to take one of them, but I wasn't sure which way to go.

Leaves rustled behind me, causing the hair on the back of my neck to stand up.

I turned around.

A dark figure lunged toward me with a sword. I didn't have anything to block it with. Fire exploded. I shielded my eyes from the blast and the heat spread over my body, threatening to burn me alive.

I woke up sweating, frantically searching the dark room. I was still on the couch. The TV was off. My heart rate slowed, and my breathing returned to normal.

It wasn't real.

But it certainly felt like it was.

Checking the time, I realized I had accidentally slept through the night. School wouldn't start for another hour, but I needed something to do to distract me from that nightmare. I walked around the couch and through the kitchen to my room. The green dresser creaked as I yanked it open, pulling out a color-splattered shirt and a pair of jean shorts. I slipped on my sneakers, grabbed my backpack, and headed out the door.

The dream stayed on my mind throughout the day. The injuries, the fire, the surroundings, all of it felt way too real. Anytime I heard a rustle behind me, someone shifting in their desk, the dark figure entered my mind, making me jumpy. I was so focused on not thinking about it that I barely paid attention to what was going on around me.

Before I knew it, I stared at the food choices in the lunch line. Everything smelled processed, so I grabbed a salad, exited the line, and looked for an empty tablet. A blur of a person ran in front of me. I retracted my foot and took a couple short steps back. A tray bumped into my back.

"Sorry," I apologized as I turned around. His milk carton and pudding cup had fallen over on his tray. A pair of wide, green eyes looked back at me. "Greyson."

"I'm sorry, Elisia. I didn't see you there," he responded, even though it was my fault.

"It's alright. I should've watched where I was going" A smile rose to my lips.

His lips parted to speak but then closed tightly.

Someone called his name, and he looked away. A guy with dark brown hair that seemed almost black and deep blue eyes stood next to a filled table, waving him over. Noah. Greyson nodded, then turned back to me.

I took a step away from him. "I better go."

"Why don't you sit with us?" he asked.

My heart jumped at the offer, but my brain froze.

"You're going to the pool party, right?"

I nodded.

"This way you can meet some people that'll be there." He scratched the back of his head.

I thought for a second, but before my brain could process what was happening, I spoke.

"Sure."

What did I just say?

I mentally yelled at myself before I followed him over to the table of football players and cheerleaders.

Though I recognized a couple of people from gym class, I didn't know the others. They were the popular kids, the ones I never really tried to get to know—too much attention from others. And attention wasn't a good thing. Not when I wasn't all human.

For most of lunch, I sat quietly eating beside Greyson, listening to the endless conversations about football and parties.

Noah said my name.

I jumped, looking up at him with a mouthful.

"Elisia, you live on the outside of town, just down the road from me, right?" He paused so I could answer him.

I nodded, still mid-chew.

"So, you live on the edge of the Dead Zone too, right? You ever think about having a Halloween party in your backyard? I had one last year, but, um, it didn't exactly go as planned."

Everyone laughed.

I faked a chuckle.

I hated the name, the "Dead Zone." People gave it that name because of how many people entered the forest and went missing. Humans knew stories of Perfidious, but since the first days of its existence, Perfidious had become just that—stories. No one really believed in monsters or that they could live so close to them.

I swallowed my food. "No, I guess I never did."

"Well, I think you—Ouch!" Noah stopped, looking up at Greyson on the other side of me.

"Sorry," Greyson spoke up. "Noah has parties on the mind all the time. He hosts fifty parties a year at our house, and I don't think I wanna know how many parties he's influenced other people to have."

Noah swallowed a mouthful and pointed his fork at Greyson. "You're one to talk. Where do you think I get half my ideas?"

Greyson looked down at his tray, his lips twitching like he was trying not to snicker. I laughed with everyone, a real laugh. The smiles around me made me feel warm. It was nice hanging out with humans, pretending I was normal.

After lunch, the day flew by in a haze. My mind was preoccupied, thinking about the party. *What would I wear? Should I wear clothes there or just my bathing suit?*

I went from class to class, just going through the motions. Butterflies swarmed around my insides. I'd heard a lot about how rowdy Noah's parties could get and was probably in over my head, especially since it was the first party I'd been invited to. But I was still excited to go.

Just like I was excited to spar with Kalvin and my new sword.

After the last bell, I made my usual route home, heading around the house, throwing my backpack inside through my window, and jogging into the woods. Kalvin waited for me outside my cellar. I waved at him as I grabbed the sword, but I was too anxious to chat.

A sword came down at my face.

I reacted quickly, throwing my right arm up to block the impact.

Kalvin stopped the swing inches from my bare arm. I looked at the scene and realized my sword was in my other hand. He removed the dangerous blade and gracefully returned it to his side.

"I could'a taken your arm off," Kalvin stated, using his teacher voice. "Using the blade as an extension of your arm doesn't mean *use your arm*."

"I know. I know." I stuck the sword into the ground. A little too hard. "Ugh! I'm used to combat, both hands. I can't do this. I'm not cut out for a single blade. Can't I just train with something like your daggers?"

"Daggers have short blades, and you don't have protective dragon skin like I do." He shifted his weight, studying me. "You were so excited about this, Elisia. Where's your mind at? Cause it's definitely not sparring with me." He paused, and a smirk rose to his lips. "If I'm such a distraction, then we shouldn't train together anymore."

I had to look away from his piercing eyes. "No, that's not it. I don't like the one-handed style. I'm used to using the other person's momentum against them. I like having two weapons." I held up my two fists but dropped them in a wide gesture. "Don't you have anything that I can combine my combat with instead of completely learning a new style? Got anything else I can hold in both hands, instead of daggers?"

"Hmm..." He shifted his weight and stroked his nonexistent beard. "I'll take ya to my mom's tomorrow. I'm sure she'll have an idea on what you should use." His smirk grew mischievous as he eyed me up and down. "I know that with a body like yours, ya can be deadly with just your fist." His expression turned serious again. "However, I also think ya should have some sort of blade, especially with the way Perfidious is."

"Kalvin, I can't go tomorrow. I have plans..."

He raised an eyebrow.

"Some of my classmates invited me to a party," I explained.

"Interesting. What kinda party?" Disappointment laced his empty tone, but he never let it show in his features. He set his sword on the ground.

"A pool party. It's with a bunch of humans, though, so my mom's gonna help me cover up my Anchor. I don't want anyone to ask questions about it." I sat down on an old tree stump with a split that broke off in two parts, making it almost look like a destroyed couch.

Kalvin sat next to me, and together we watched the streams of light through the trees starting to dim. The sun was close to setting. I elbowed him and he grinned, lowering his head. His black hair hung in front just above his brow, but he never let it get long enough to cover his eyes completely.

"I should probably head back soon. I'm exhausted," I said, looking up and resting the back of my head on the longer part of the tree.

"Wanna work on combat and sleep at your place tonight?" He turned his head to look at me.

I didn't need to think about it. "Sure, why not? I'll text my mom to let her know."

I got up and sent a quick text to Mom, planting my feet to prepare for his "surprise" attack.

His smile grew and then vanished.

Kalvin stood and, in one swift motion, aimed a punch directly at my stomach. I jumped back and got into a fighting stance as we circled one another, waiting for someone to make the first move.

4

Sun rays peeked through a crack in the roots above me. I rolled to my side on the soft mattress, pulling the covers over my head. On the verge of falling back asleep, my eyes flew open.

If the sun was high enough to peer through the roots, I'd be late for school. I tossed the covers to the side and flew out of bed.

Sadly, my foot caught a lump on the floor, and my body became a victim to gravity. I fell face first into the hard dirt. I turned over, planning to kick the lump for tripping me.

Kalvin's sleeping face stopped me. I forgot he stayed over the night before. He sprawled out on his usual bed whenever he visited, a spare mattress on the floor, softly smiling in his sleep and showing no signs of waking. I let out a breath I didn't know I was holding. He usually wasn't the kindest person in the morning.

Well, neither was I, but I could not be late. Not that day, anyway. If Greyson noticed I wasn't at school, he might take back his invitation, and I was looking forward to the party. I quickly changed my clothes around the corner of the circular L-shaped area where Kalvin couldn't see if he woke up. I rummaged through my bag to make sure I had everything.

Check.

I reached for the door, my palm encircling the knob—

A pair of arms reached around my neck.

My body tightened, ready to jab an elbow into the attacker's rib cage on reflex.

Kalvin's sleep-filled voice tickled my ear. "Ya should stay." He rested his chin on the top of my head. "I don't want ya to leave."

"Kalvin," I sighed. I grabbed his arm and flipped him over my shoulder. He crashed on the ground in front of me in a millisecond.

He had to raise his voice over my laughter for me to hear. "Why must you torture me?" His toothy grin mocked me, not even phased by the impact. Stupid dragon skin.

"Oh, please. You're such a shameless flirt. I have to go to school. I'll be back later to spend the night. We're going to Tamara's early." I smiled back.

"I remember. Well," he said, propping his head up with his arms, "I'll wait in this exact spot for ya."

I placed a hand on my hip as I made sure I didn't need anything else. "There's no food here."

He got up, fast as a blur. "On second thought, I'll wait at my place."

We both climbed out of the cellar and said our good-byes before I ran to my house. I quietly grabbed my back-pack from the place inside my window before running to school. The ten-minute walk took me about two minutes. I didn't care who saw me.

The bell rang as I rounded the corner to my math classroom. My empty seat in the back row was only about five or six steps away, but I couldn't see if the teacher was looking towards the class or the white board.

Greyson still sat in the seat next to mine.

I waved to get his attention. His eyes caught mine, an amused smirk spreading across his face. Then, he raised his hand.

It confused me, but I had to trust that he wasn't ratting on me.

Mrs. Walker asked what he needed.

"Could you write the extended form of number three on the board? I'm confused on how the order should be."

I heard the shuffling of feet from the teacher. Greyson looked my way, motioning me to come in, so I quickly tiptoed my way to the desk. Mrs. Walker continued writing on the board, and I pulled out my book, opening it to a random page.

I turned to look at Greyson, mouthing the words *thank you*. He replied with a short head nod before returning his attention to the board.

Mrs. Walker turned around to speak to the class, grazing over me. She closed her mouth and narrowed her eyes. "Ms. Meyer."

I stiffened.

"Did you just sneak in here?"

I gave her my most innocent look. "No, I've been here the entire time."

Her features hardened as she placed her hands on the pattern of oversized flowers covering her hip. "Then explain why this is the first time I've seen you today."

I tried not to show my pride. "Have you put your

glasses on yet?" I had used the excuse more than once that year but in different situations. I was so glad that it hadn't failed me.

She looked like she went to push up her glasses, finding they weren't there. She grunted and returned to the lesson.

Greyson leaned towards me. "You need to teach me how to do that to Mr. Hobbins."

I snickered silently and whispered back. "Just tell him his motorcycle distracted you on the way in. He loves to talk about the importance of a good automobile for the entire class period."

He smiled as though what I said was the most obvious answer in the world.

"We're on page 124," he said as I flipped through my book.

"Thanks."

I watched the clock tick by, counting away the day. By the time gym came around, my impatience to leave school and get ready for the party had become unbearable.

I rushed home before the final bell had stopped ringing. As soon as I jumped through my window, I removed my clothes and slid into my purple bikini. The top looked like an infinity sign, crisscrossing in the middle of my chest, and the bottoms had the same pattern on the sides.

Mom walked in to check on me. "Are you sure there won't be any alcohol there?"

"Yes, Mom. No alcohol."

She made me sit down as she applied makeup to cover up my Anchor. "This thing is always so hard to cover up. It's pretty, and you can pretend it's just a normal tattoo. Why don't you just let people see it?"

I furrowed my brow and turned down the corners of my mouth, my voice becoming quieter. "I hate it when humans ask me about it. It's easier to cover my Anchor with makeup than answer questions with lies."

Mom wrapped her arms around me, pulling my gaze to her reflection in the mirror. "Well, I'm a human, and I love both parts of you. Who knows, maybe you'll meet some people at the party that you could open up to."

I loved her optimism, but her carefree attitude was something I never understood. I hugged her and stood up. "And you're sure that I don't have to make dinner or do extra chores tonight?"

"Let's just say our agreement is on hold for tonight," she said as she handed me my rainbow cover up.

I wrapped it around me and tied it at my waist, checking my appearance in the mirror one last time. To most humans, I looked exotic, but I loved my unusually bright features. It was the only visual hint that I was part elf, besides my Anchor.

But the makeup concealed it, showing just a normal shoulder. I would still need to be careful and avoid getting my upper half wet. The makeup wasn't waterproof.

I walked out the front door and started down the road to Noah and Greyson's house.

5

Music reached my ears before I had even made it to the driveway. The open front door beckoned me inside the two-story house. A huge crowd of people, most of them I recognized from school, already loitered in the rooms and hallways. The bass pulsed through my body as I maneuvered through the crowds to the pool.

Less people were in the backyard. Some swam in the pool or sat around the edge, dangling their feet in, but most stood in small groups scattered around the backyard. Everyone seemed like they were having a good time, but my eyes were searching for Greyson.

Someone tapped me on the shoulder.

"Hey, Elisia. When did you get here?" Noah greeted me, handing me a drink. His hair seemed browner in the sunlight.

I raised my eyebrows and looked hesitantly from the red plastic cup back to Noah's face.

His smile grew. "I only serve the hard stuff at night

parties. But I would still be careful. This is some strong strawberry punch."

"I just got here a minute ago," I answered his original question as I took a sip. "Wow, this has a lot of sugar in it."

"Too much? Greyson can go overboard sometimes." He chuckled, flashing perfectly white teeth.

"No, not too much. Just a surprise."

"Think you'll enjoy yourself, first-timer?"

"Yeah, and it seems like I'm not the only one." I avoided a splash from someone jumping into the pool. "It looks like the entire high school is here, plus some."

He took the compliment instantly, and his eyes gleamed with pride.

"Speaking of people, is Greyson here yet?" I asked.

"Well, considering he lives here, yeah." He pointed to a group of muscular guys across the yard as he took a sip from his cup. "He's right there—the one in the sunset shorts. Well, I gotta go play host." Noah gave me a genuine grin. "Let me know if you need anything."

I walked toward the group Noah had pointed out, looking for Greyson. It was hard to tell which one was him until I spotted the sunset swim trunks. The person next to him shifted slightly, bringing more of a shirtless Greyson into my view.

Shock shivered down my spine, stopping me dead in my tracks.

Greyson had a tattoo on his left shoulder. Dark grey ink stood out against his tan skin, a circle with a triangle inside of it with another triangle inside of that, but the second triangle was upside down. The mark shimmered, and I knew.

It was an Anchor.

A sinking feeling grew in the pit of my stomach, but I did my best to collect my composure, making sure no one saw me staring at him. Greyson laughed at something before I tapped on his shoulder. He turned around and met my gaze.

He beamed with surprise. "Hey, Elisia, I almost thought you wouldn't show up."

"I told you I was coming, didn't I?" I smiled slightly, but my mind stayed focused on the Anchor.

"Yes, you did." He pivoted back to his group. "I'll catch up with you guys later."

I got another quick glance at Greyson's mark, still with the distinctive shimmer. My heart fell; I had hoped I was just seeing things.

When he turned back around, my eyes shot to his. We would have to talk about it, but I didn't want it to be awkward. Him noticing me staring at it would definitely make it awkward.

"Greyson, can we talk?" I asked, somehow sounding more serious than I intended.

His brow creased. "Sure?"

"Alone," I added, throwing a quick glance to the group of guys still within earshot.

Greyson frowned but led me to the other side of Noah's backyard. The house bordered the pool in an L-shape, so we didn't have to go far to escape human ears.

Once I knew we were out of hearing distance, I dropped my act. "That's an interesting Anchor. I've never seen an insignia like that. What does it mean?"

Greyson looked confused. "What's an Anchor?"

"Greyson, I know that isn't just a tattoo," I spoke slowly.

He probably thought I was human. I usually tried to keep my Anchor covered at school, so he most likely hadn't seen it before, unless he spent time in the girl's locker room.

"Wait, so, you wanted to talk alone about my tattoo?" Greyson broke eye contact as he lowered his chin.

"Yeah. I didn't think you'd want others to overhear our conversation."

He was being overly secretive about it for no reason. I called it an Anchor. He should have caught on that I knew about Perfidious.

"Yeah, okay? Um...I don't know what it means. I was so nervous about getting a tattoo, I don't remember," he responded, acting the same way I did when someone asked about mine.

"You can drop the act. I know you didn't 'get it' from a person."

A puzzled look in his eyes stopped me from saying anything else. My eyes widened as the realization struck me.

He didn't know what I was talking about.

My brain wasn't working, but my mouth acted on its own. "Wait a minute...you really don't know?"

"Know what?" Greyson asked. He scratched the back of his head, but his face relaxed and his mouth opened slightly.

I stared into Greyson's green eyes, full of questions. But if he really didn't know, I didn't want to be the one to tell him, dragging him into the same situation as I was in. Telling him would split his world in two and bring him more danger than not knowing would. I had just started hanging out with him. I didn't want to ruin his life. He was too good of a person for Perfidious.

Greyson took a step towards me, and I found that I couldn't remove my gaze from his eyes. Their green color reminded me of the moss that covered the trees in Perfidious. A wave of calm washed over me.

Should I tell him? He really doesn't know about all this. I could just—

Someone cleared their throat next to us. I took a step back from Greyson, and Noah took a couple hesitant steps forward.

"Sorry to interrupt," Noah apologized. "Elisia, can I borrow Greyson for a moment? It will be quick. I promise."

I gladly took the escape. "No problem," I said, forcing a smile.

When I turned to head back to the party, Greyson took a couple steps to follow me, but Noah put his hand on his chest. I rounded the corner, out of sight, and pushed back my hair.

Why did Noah intervene? Did he know? They did live together. Maybe Greyson confided in him.

I didn't intend to eavesdrop. It just happened.

"Hey!" Noah shouted at Greyson, then softened his voice with concern. "What was that all about?"

"She was asking me about my birthmark, Noah." Greyson sounded confused.

"What exactly does Elisia know?" Noah said, as if me knowing was a bad thing.

"Something." The hopefulness in Greyson's voice broke my heart. "She thought I knew too, but..." Greyson paused. "But how would she know what it is?"

There was silence for a couple seconds.

"Do you think she has one?" he finally asked.

"If she does, it's covered, or it's not on her shoulder. I didn't see one there earlier," Noah said. Noah's voice grew louder, more confident. "Don't worry, Greyson. If she knows anything, I'll find out."

It didn't exactly sound like a threat—more like a promise.

I quickly returned to the crowd before they realized I was listening to the conversation.

I spent the next hour talking with people about school and football, but I really didn't pay attention to any of it. Most of the time, I just listened.

My mind spun with so many thoughts.

What would I do if he cornered me? I couldn't lie to another half-breed, though I found it hard to believe he didn't know. Was he lying to me?

How would something like that happen anyway? It wasn't like monsters could really hide what they were. Most of them stayed within the borders of Perfidious. They all knew they'd be outnumbered if another war started up. All monsters would be wiped out for sure.

I shook my head and took a sip of punch. To calm down and distract myself, I started a conversation with one of the football players I met during lunch the day before. He started talking about his muscles, and I kept nodding like I was listening, but my mind was more focused on keeping Noah in my peripherals. It concerned me that he said he would find out, and I wanted to be ready if he tried something.

A couple hours later, I realized Noah had done nothing to find out what I knew. He never talked to me after that, and Greyson barely even looked at me. He was also a host, so I guess he had to make the rounds along with Noah.

Overreacting. I was just overreacting.

I made the quick decision to talk to Kalvin about Greyson before I made any rash decisions. He would probably know a better way to approach the situation.

When other people began to leave to go home, I began to look for Noah or Greyson to let them know I was leaving and to thank them for the party. However, as I walked around a crowd of people, an elbow pressed into my arm, pushing me back. My feet connected with the edge of the pool.

I gasped.

For a moment, my body seemed suspended in mid-air.

I hit the water hard, my bare back stinging from the impact. Consumed by the water, I instinctively held my breath and closed my eyes, flailing my arms and legs to get out. Breaking through the surface, I coughed as I tried to take in too much oxygen at one time. I moved to the stairs.

Noah stood on the third step of the entrance into the water. My shock faded.

"You okay? I saw you fall in," Noah asked, concern written on his face...along with something else.

"I'm fine," I said, wringing out my hair as I got out of the pool.

He smirked. "Follow me. You can use one of my beach towels."

I followed him into the house. Noah put his hand on my left shoulder as he led me up the stairs to a closet near a bathroom. He handed me a towel, and I wrapped it around me, glancing at my shoulder. My Anchor was becoming visible. I made a mental note to get some water-proof concealer and turned around.

Noah just stood there with his arms crossed.

In that moment, I realized Noah might be more clever than I gave him credit for. His hand on my left shoulder flashed through my mind. He had thought to try to wipe off any makeup that might have been there. He probably pushed me into the pool, too. I seriously underestimated the guy.

"So, I overheard you talking to Greyson about his tattoo. You're acting like it was the key to a secret club or something." He spoke accusingly, yet he acted like he was telling a joke.

"I mistook it as something else," I said, trying to play the game. "Thanks for the towel. Do you mind if I borrow it? I only live down the road."

"Sure," he said, frowning. I turned to walk away, but he spoke up before I could descend the stairs. "Elisia?"

I turned around to see his face, more serious than before.

"Let's cut the crap," he continued. "You hid a *tattoo* with makeup, asked Greyson strange questions about *his* tattoo. I'm assuming you know something, and if I'm right, you should tell him. It's been driving him crazy his entire life."

A risky move. He was outright confronting me. Did they even know anything about the Anchor? I imagined how I'd feel if I never knew about my elf side, or if I was born with a strange tattoo no one was able to explain. I could have played the dumb card, but I felt very conflicted about not telling him.

"You're his friend. What if it's something he'd prefer to not know?" I countered. It'd be a lot for him to carry on his shoulders. His life would no longer be normal. "What if it put him in danger?"

"Knowledge isn't harmful. What people do with it is. Either way, he deserves to know." Noah stood tall, a glimmer in his eye. It was the first time I ever saw Noah that serious. He knew he was right.

So did I.

I bit my lip as I stopped to think. Whether I told him or not, I knew I'd regret whatever decision I made. I just hoped he could handle the truth.

"Fine," I exhaled. "I'll talk to him later."

Noah didn't like my answer. "No, after the party. All three of us can sit down, and then you can fill in the gaps for us."

It would probably be a while until everyone left. *That would give me plenty of time to figure out what I can say. Or what I should say.*

"Okay. Fine. But only after everyone leaves. I don't want anyone overhearing us."

Noah's toothy grin mocked me as he turned and started making his way down the stairs. I didn't like the look he had on his face, so I followed him through the maze of people crowding the living room in front of the stereo. Noah turned the dial that controlled the music, and the room fell into a hushed quiet. Noah got on top of a chair and clapped his hands to get everyone's attention.

"What are you doing?" I whispered to him.

Noah ignored me and spoke to the crowd. "Sorry, everyone, this has been an awesome party, but I have to cut it short." He paused. Everyone started speaking at once. "I just got a call from my parents. They finished work early and will be here in an hour."

I watched the different reactions to the impending arrival of the parents. Some people immediately started for the door while others just looked disappointed.

Noah got down from the chair and joined me.

"What are you doing? I said after the party," I whispered to him.

"I know. And the party's over. Now, about that tattoo?"

6

I t didn't take long for Greyson to find us.

"What's going on?" Greyson asked as a wave of partiers moved around him, heading for the door.

Before Noah could reply, someone came up behind us. Muscular, blonde hair, cute. Anthony from gym class carried a stack of dirty cups.

"Noah, where's the garbage bags?" he asked.

Noah never dropped his everything-is-fine look. "You guys don't need to help. Greyson, Elisia, and I can take care of it. Elisia lives closer than you guys, and I don't want you involved if my parents show up earlier than they said."

A guy to the left of Anthony made a face. "Yeah, your mom can be pretty scary when she wants to be. Are you sure you can clean it all up in time?"

"Yeah, we've got it handled. See you on Monday." Noah said goodbye as he pushed them out of the house.

Greyson was still dumbfounded, waiting for an answer. "Elisia, what's going on?"

"Noah's being a sneaky jerk," I answered as I watched Noah rush the last of the partygoers out the door.

The house fell silent besides the whispered conversation between Greyson and Noah. I sat in a chair as I thought about what I would say. My entire life, I had been learning things about the world of monsters, but Greyson and Noah didn't need to know everything right then. I needed to keep it to the point and answer as many questions as I could without scaring him.

They walked over to join me in the living room. Greyson still looked unsure as Noah spoke. "Tell him."

They sat down, but Greyson's eyes stayed locked on me, a mix of emotions in that one look.

"How long have you had your 'tattoo'?" I asked him, just wanting to clarify.

Greyson's eyes looked strong, unwilling to give up his secret that easily, but I continued to look at him with soft eyes, so he knew that I meant no harm.

He sighed and his body visibly relaxed. "I've had it all my life. Noah thought it might have been genetic, but I don't remember my mom having one." His voice lowered. "Not that I remember much about her."

"Okay. Um. You're not that far off. It's a type of birthmark called an Anchor." I paused. *How could I explain?* It wasn't like I was trying to tell him he was secretly German or Irish or something. I leaned forward. "Everyone...like us...has one."

My lips thinned. *Way to go, Elisia. How stupidly cryptic of you.*

"Everyone like us? But I didn't think you had a tattoo... or Anchor...or whatever it is," Greyson said, still confused.

Noah scooted closer to Greyson and put his hand on

his shoulder. "I asked some girls from our gym class. Cassie saw it the other day. She covered it up with makeup for the party."

To confirm what Noah was saying, I turned around in my seat and rubbed off what remained of the makeup covering my Anchor. I heard Greyson inhale sharply and could tell by the look in his eyes he knew it was different.

"Our Anchors are formed when human blood mixes with monster blood in the womb. The mark signifies you're not all human." I paused, allowing Greyson to process what I was saying, but his facial expression didn't change.

"If I'm not human, then what am I?" he asked, looking down at his hands as though they weren't his anymore.

The flatness in his voice shocked me. He was taking in all that I was saying, listening fully. That cemented my decision. I wouldn't hold back any information, no matter the truth. He would believe me, or he wouldn't.

"I don't know. It's not an exact science. Anchors can have similarities between species, but other than that, all Anchors are different. It's hard to tell unless you show it to someone that knows all about Anchor designs."

"Is there really no other way to know?" Greyson asked, slouching against the couch, sinking into the cushions.

He still wasn't making eye contact with Noah or me.

"I mean, the Coalfell Elders might have more information? I'm sorry, Greyson. I've never dealt with anything like this."

I felt bad. He came to me, thinking I would have all the answers, but I was only bringing him more questions. I shook my head. He probably didn't know what I meant by Elders either.

"There's a panel of half-breed Elders that run a nearby village called Coalfell, just inside Perfidious."

"Perfidious? Coalfell?" Noah scoffed, acting like it was all a joke. He leaned forward with mocking eyes. "Where is this magical land? I would love to visit. Is it nearby?"

My hands clenched as I moved to the edge of my seat. "This isn't a joke, Noah. I'm telling the truth." And also getting mildly irritated. "Why do you think so many people go missing in the Dead Zone? It's because they're killed by the monsters. They enter through the gates and can't find their way back."

Greyson finally brought his head up. He looked over at Noah, whose grin lessened but didn't completely fall.

Noah raised his hands palms-up. "What? I'm sorry, Greyson, but she's lying. I thought she could've told you something useful. I guess I was wrong for once."

Greyson opened his mouth to say something, but Noah cut him off. "I'm just saying I don't believe her. She says you and her are part *monster*?" He turned to glare at me. "You both look *human* to me."

"It depends on the genes, dumbass. I'm half-elf, which means I would appear mostly human anyway. I just didn't inherit my father's looks, like the pointed ears." I was getting really annoyed with Noah, so I turned my attention to Greyson who looked deep in thought. "It's a lot to process. I know." I stood, ready to leave. "But if you choose to not believe me, that's on you."

Greyson stood up next to me. He smiled, but it seemed more nervous than excited.

"'Nothing is impossible.' It's the only thing I remember about my biological mom. She always told me that before she died." He scratched his head and snuck a peek at Noah before looking back at me. "Will you take me to see the Coalfell Elders? If they have the resources to answer more of my questions, then I want to speak to them. Is there a way we can talk to them tonight?"

I hesitated, still unsure if it was the best idea to bring him into my world. "Possibly...? We'd have to see if they're available. Or we could always just go tomorrow. Coalfell isn't too far away, about fifteen minutes on foot."

Greyson shook his head. "I want to speak with them tonight. If they aren't, is there somewhere we can stay the night? That way we can talk to them first thing in the morning."

"It's really not far. We wouldn't have to stay the night." I countered, taking a step back.

But Greyson was persistent. "I'd rather talk to them as soon as possible."

Noah got up to stop us from going anywhere. "Not without me you're not. I want to see proof that you're telling the truth."

I snapped my head in his direction at his suggestion. "No. You'll attract too much attention."

Noah crossed his arms and looked down at me. "What? Are humans not allowed in this fantasy world of yours?"

"I didn't say that, but only a handful of humans know about monsters and how to enter Perfidious. It's not exactly safe—"

"Then, I'm going, and you can't stop me." Noah crossed his arms.

I took a step forward, ready to show him just how wrong he was, but I stepped right into Greyson.

"Elisia, he's coming with us. He's like my brother, and he's helped me figure this out so far. I want him there."

I peered around Greyson at Noah's smug face, then looked back to Greyson. His expression was soft, but his stance was strong. Neither one of them backed down.

"It's his death wish. Perfidious isn't safe for humans." I started walking to the door. "Anyway, I'm gonna go home to change and come right back. Then, we'll leave."

I went home to change into jeans and a sweater. Mom caught me as I was heading out for the second time.

"Where do you think you're going?" she asked, her arms crossed.

"It's really important, Mom," I begged. "I don't really have time to explain."

"That didn't answer my question." Her foot tapping echoed down the hallway.

"To Coalfell." I called back to her as I put my shoes on. "I'm going with a friend to talk to the Elders, then probably staying at Kalvin's. Is that okay?"

Mom was silent for what seemed like forever. "Fine. As long as you are with Kalvin. Text me if anything changes."

I nodded and was out the door before she could change her mind.

Noah and Greyson were sitting on the front porch waiting for me. I motioned them to follow, and Greyson practically skipped down the stairs to my side.

Shadows consumed the forest behind Noah's house, but there was plenty of light to see where we were going. It didn't matter that I didn't have a path to follow or a compass to guide me. I knew where I was going.

"Hey, Greyson," Noah whispered, breaking the silence. "Did it ever cross your mind that she's taking us out here to kill us?"

"No, why would it?" Greyson snapped back. He kept

his eyes forward, stepping over underbrush and broken tree limbs.

Noah shrugged. "I'm just saying. We've been walking for almost five minutes now, and we're heading to the area that's impassable."

I grinned at Noah's comment. "That's because it's spelled. People can only get into Perfidious if they go through a gate. Otherwise, it just seems like extremely thick foliage."

"Wait," Noah chuckled, "you're telling me there are wizards now too?"

I glared at him. "No, I'm saying it's *spelled*. Druids used to exist that could perform some sort of magic, but druids haven't been seen since Perfidious was created."

Noah rolled his eyes and whispered, "Convenient."

We reached one of the few gates meant for half-breeds and humans to cross into the borders of Perfidious, the only one I'd ever been through. The boys' reactions differed. Noah raised his eyebrows, but our eyes met, and his face immediately returned his neutral expression.

On the other hand, Greyson stared ahead with wide eyes at the tree nymphs dancing between the trunks. They always liked to hang out around the gates, hoping to hear some human music.

We only had about half a mile between the gate and the edge of the village.

Greyson and Noah mostly argued quietly behind me while we walked. I tried not to listen. It felt like I was a tour guide or something with how they were reacting. But when we reached the main shopping area of town, they both fell silent.

Little lean-tos lined up on both sides of the path,

creating places for merchants to set up their shops. Most of them appeared to be closing up for the day.

Many of the half-breeds we passed didn't look human. I rolled my eyes at Greyson and Noah who were staring, jaws dropped, at a fairy-elf half-breed. Noah pointed at the wings that resembled the orange and yellow tones of a butterfly, but the half-breed's height and pointed ears gave away his elf side.

Noah's eyes met mine. He stopped gawking and gave me a toothy grin.

"Elisia?" Greyson mumbled. "How many of you are there? Are there a lot of different species of creatures?" He was stumbling over his words, and I tried not to giggle at him.

I turned slightly so he could hear me. "There used to be a lot more, but over time, some have become extinct."

He seemed to be too busy looking around to respond.

An old ogre, with more wrinkles than smooth skin, passed us. His arms almost dragged the ground as he walked because of their length.

Greyson leaned in to whisper in my ear. "What is he?"

I responded, my voice lowering to match his. "I think he's an ogre, but it's not always easy to tell. There's mostly half-breeds here, but there are some purebloods too."

"How can you tell a difference?"

"Sometimes you can't. Half-breeds that are half-human have the Anchors, but half-breeds that have two halves of different monsters don't have anything like that to identify them."

He furrowed his brow. "Why is that?"

"I'm not sure. Some say it's the way the Gods like to

mark us as impure, but I don't think anyone really knows why we're born with marks and they aren't."

We continued toward the center of Coalfell. The lean-tos turned into houses, but the houses in Perfidious looked more like cottages compared to the giant houses normal humans have in the city. Walking into Perfidious made me feel like I was going back in time compared to the human town I lived in. Pathways made of dirt and stones helped the residents travel instead of roads. Most traveled by wings, on foot, or by animal, instead of by car.

After multiple rows of houses, we reached a giant teepee in the center of town. The guards that normally stood outside were gone, and I could hear no movement. I peeked inside just to make sure they were gone.

I turned around, shaking my head at Greyson's hopeful eyes. His face fell.

"We can come back tomorrow morning. Are you guys sure you don't want to go home?" I said, giving them a second chance to go back home for the night.

"No. I want to be close by." Greyson decided. He looked at Noah to check with him, and Noah nodded.

"Okay. Follow me. I'll introduce you to a friend of mine. We'll stay with him tonight."

Kalvin lived closer to the edge of town. He didn't like to be in the middle of all the commotion of the village. I walked up to the familiar door and knocked. Inside, I heard the shuffle of feet, and Kalvin opened the door, wearing a red shirt that showed his abs through the fabric and a pair of black sweats.

Kalvin gave me a charming smile as he leaned his forearm on the wooden door frame above his head. "Ya here to take my offer?" Then his nose twitched. He looked behind me and sighed. Kalvin straightened his back and folded his arms over his chest. "What'd ya do?"

I gasped and punched him in the chest. He pretended it hurt, but I knew punching him hurt my hand more than his chest.

"What makes you think I did anything?"

"You have a human and a—" he paused and noticeably sniffed the air, "—something else with you. When have you ever brought any of your little human friends here?"

"Point taken. Kalvin, this is Noah, the human, and Greyson. Greyson needs to speak to the Elders, who have already left for the night. I need a place for them to stay, so I can take them early tomorrow." I gave him puppy dog eyes, hoping he would say yes.

Kalvin's face fell. "You know how dangerous this could be?" His eyes shifted to Greyson, his pupils narrowing. "What is he, anyway? His scent is strange."

"See...about that...he doesn't exactly know." I was lucky that I was Kalvin's best friend. By the look he gave me, I knew he would never do it for anyone else. "Please, Kalvin."

Defeated, Kalvin stepped to the side for us to enter. "Will you be joinin' us?" he asked, assessing Greyson and Noah.

"Yeah, I'll stay. I don't trust you all alone together." I nodded at him as I walked in.

"Well," Kalvin sighed. "Ya know where the extra blankets are, and the couch unfolds. Are ya sleeping out here, or do ya wanna cuddle in my bed?" His eyes flickered to Greyson.

I'm not sure why he mentioned cuddling. We'd never done anything like that before. At the cellar, he always took the floor. I'd only slept there a few times, but that was when Aaron was still alive. I slept on the couch back then.

"Um, I'll sleep on the floor. I'm not gonna take your bed," I answered him.

"Okay. I'll be in my room." He walked through the door to the kitchen and around to his bedroom.

Greyson watched Kalvin leave, his face void of emotion, while Noah's eyes darted between us.

"Sorry about him. He's not a big fan of people." I wiped my sweaty hands on my leggings.

Noah broke the awkward silence that was beginning to build. "So, what is he? Is he an elf like you?"

"No, he's half-human, half-dragon."

Noah's eyes widened.

Greyson moved to the couch. "Is he your boyfriend?"

"Kalvin?" I almost choked on air. "No, no. Not my boyfriend. He's just my best friend." I shifted uncomfortably. Time to change the subject. "Are you guys good sharing the couch?" I grabbed the extra blankets from the closet.

Greyson looked down at the couch and started taking off the cushions. "We'll be fine."

"Okay. I'm gonna go talk to him," I said, walking towards Kalvin's room.

I knocked on his bedroom door. He was moving around inside but didn't answer. I entered anyway.

"Hey," I whispered.

"Did you really have to bring them here?" He didn't look at me, just continued throwing a couple of blankets and a pillow on the floor.

"They asked to stay in the village. I thought you'd be okay with it," I said, closing the door.

"Yup. Completely okay with ya bringing two guys here from your little human party," he snapped. Then, he turned back to me and his features softened. "I didn't mean it like that. I'm just...tired. I didn't sleep the best last night."

I nodded. He crawled into the bed he made on the floor and pulled the covers over his head.

"Aren't you going to get into bed?" I asked.

"I did," he responded.

I opened my mouth to say something, but he didn't let me speak.

"I'm not going to make ya sleep on the floor. Just get into the bed and go to sleep."

I smiled in the darkness. "Thanks Kalvin. I owe you one."

"More like three," he whispered.

Without another word, I crawled under the covers and went to sleep.

7

In the morning, I didn't waste any time. As soon as I saw the sun, I threw my feet over the edge of the bed, careful not to hit Kalvin who was still fast asleep on the floor. I tiptoed to his bathroom in the hallway and looked at myself in the mirror. My eyes took a second to adjust to the bright light. I splashed some water on my face.

"Not a morning person?" someone said behind me.

My heart stopped. I whipped around, ready to punch whatever was behind me.

Noah glared at me.

"Don't sneak up on me like that!" I told him after I found my lungs again.

Noah stood in the doorway laughing at me. "How did I sneak up on you? Don't you have superhuman hearing?"

"You didn't. I do. You just—I'm not awake, and the water was running. Okay?" I didn't want him knowing he scared me.

"Ha! I totally scared the shit out of you."

Well, so much for that.

I rolled my eyes. "Yeah, yeah. Get Greyson. We're leaving soon." I watched him leave. Although, I wished I'd wiped the smirk from his face.

I finished getting ready and went into the living room, expecting to find Greyson just waking up. Instead, he paced around the room. The pullout bed was already put back into the couch, and he was folding the last blanket.

"Greyson?"

No answer.

"Greyson?" I asked again, but that time I stepped into his line of sight.

Wow. He doesn't look like he slept at all.

His eyes snapped up to mine. "Hm?"

"Ready to go?"

He hesitated but nodded quickly.

We walked out the front door. I turned to make sure both of them were following me, but instead of two, three guys exited the house. Kalvin, hands shoved into his pockets, looked up at my questioning gaze and shrugged. I smiled and waved for Greyson and Noah to follow us. Thankfully, it wasn't a long walk from Kalvin's house to the Elders' tent.

We ended up waiting almost an hour before we received admittance to see the Elders, who had been busy dealing with the everyday concerns of Coalfell residents. Upon entering the teepee, strong waves of frankincense and myrrh assaulted my nostrils. The only light in the room came from lanterns and the sun shining through a tiny hole above. The three Elders sat comfortably in a semicircle on giant pillowed cushions, their bodies covered in dark robes so only their heads were visible.

As a mandatory requirement, all Elders came from

different villages and kept their identities secret so no one could sway them through certain monster beliefs, but there were always rumors about what kind of half-breed each was.

I bowed my head in respect, but none of them looked happy to see me.

"What is it now, Elisia?" said Enmah, the one on the right.

The only female Elder, her head appeared human with a full mane of golden hair, but the way she sat revealed some sort of animal body. My best guess was a lion or dog.

"Thank you for agreeing to meet with me," I started. They didn't reward my kindness.

In fact, they never paid attention to my input, even when I visited them with ideas of how to keep half-breeds safer, which I did frequently. Half-breeds needed simple things, like self-defense classes that I even offered to teach. My ideas required building spaces like a dojo or more housing. They always said they'd think about it, but they never brought it up again.

The Elders of Coalfell thought they were safe, safe because they were closer to the border and not many pure-bloods liked to be so close to human civilizations. So in their eyes, my ideas were pointless. But the Elders also told my father, and he adamantly turned down the idea of me working in Perfidious.

After that, I lost all respect for the Elders of Coalfell.

"Get on with it, girl!" the one in the middle, Drithro, spoke impatiently. He was scaly with fangs and slitted eyes. His head looked like the face of a snake in the shape of a human.

I made sure a smile remained on my face while

addressing them. "This is Greyson. As of yesterday, he thought he was human. I spotted his Anchor, and he quickly found out I had a similar mark. However, he has more questions than I can answer, so he's hoping you could take the time to answer some?"

I gave them a mocking bow and waited for their response. The confused Elders turned to one another, whispering.

"Elisia, darling," the one on the left, Yima, spoke before the others could open their mouths. Out of all of them, he was the one that seemed more human, even though his skin was a bright blue and his eyes tinted red. "We will try our best to address the situation. Um, which one of you is Greyson?"

I nodded for him to step forward.

Drithro motioned to a guard and turned back to Greyson. "Show the guard your Anchor. Votarog has studied the differences in Anchor species similarities."

Greyson took off his shirt as the guard approached. Votarog furrowed his brow and opened his mouth to speak, only to close his lips tightly. Then, he looked to the Elders, apologizing before he explained.

"It's nothing like I have ever seen before." Votarog turned to Greyson. "Usually, there are some qualities that could identify monster blood. For example, there is usually some kind of flame symbol within an Anchor of a dragon half-breed. I am sorry, but I do not understand what yours means. The simplicity of the circle and two triangles could represent that you have more than one type of monster blood running through your veins, but there is no way to know for certain." He looked disappointed that he couldn't help more and returned to his post by the entrance.

"Well, that's a shame," Drithro said.

Enmah nodded in agreement. "Have Elisia take him until we sort it out."

Before Yima spoke, I walked forward. "He hasn't even asked you his questions! I don't have any answers to give him—"

Someone cleared their throat harshly behind me. I figured it was Kalvin, but I didn't look to find out.

With a harsh but sweet tone, Yima pointed his attention to me. "Please take him under your wing, Elisia. We don't have any answers to give him right now. Questions that can be answered at this time should be within your own knowledge. Let us figure it out, and we will summon you once we know more."

I wanted to protest again but decided against it. If they really had no answers, there was nothing I could do.

"Thank you for seeing us. Please summon us when you have answers," I said through clenched teeth as I turned to leave.

I stomped from the teepee, townspeople scattering from my path. The Elders seeing people in a tent left little room for privacy, and I watched a game of telephone begin to play around the village.

Kalvin leaned in and whispered, "We should head to your cellar." His breath tickled my ear.

A shiver rippled down my spine, and all I could do was nod.

My eyes met Greyson's, and I gestured for him to follow. We walked out of Coalfell, past the little houses on the outskirts, deeper into the forest. I could see my oak tree, but someone grabbed my wrist, stopping me.

Greyson dragged me away from Noah and Kalvin. I was confused, but I didn't say anything. He let go of my arm once we were out of human hearing distance from them.

He roughly combed his hand through his sandy brown hair. "What's gonna happen next, Elisia? They didn't even let me ask questions! They had no way of knowing if they had answers or not!"

I placed my hand on his shoulder and tilted my head so he would meet my eyes. "I know. I'm sorry. The Elders aren't always the most reliable, but I honestly thought they would've given you something more. If you have any questions about Perfidious, Kalvin or I could answer them." I felt terrible that I wasn't able to give him more.

He took a deep breath. "When I have questions about Perfidious, I'll let you know. Right now, all of my questions are about what I am and why my mom never told me, which I guess no one can tell me that last part." He opened his mouth to say something else but closed it just as fast. He clenched his fists.

"How about I take you and Noah home? You live with them, right? Maybe Noah's parents know more? You could ask them if your mom ever said anything." I removed my hand from his shoulder.

His eyes brightened. "You're right! There's no way my mom would entrust them with me if she didn't tell them anything. I'm gonna go tell Noah." He beamed and jogged back to Noah and Kalvin.

I walked up to Kalvin and elbowed him gently. "I'm gonna take them home."

He elbowed me back. "I guess that means we ain't gonna see my mom today?" He smiled understandingly, yet his eyes remained sad.

I was about to answer him, but Greyson interrupted me.

"Can I come?"

"What?" Kalvin laughed. "No."

Greyson didn't listen to him.

"Elisia, I want to see more of this world. Noah's parents won't even be back until sometime tomorrow." Greyson suddenly seemed taller.

Kalvin frowned and shrugged his shoulders. "He's got a point. We could still go. Greyson can come as soon as we drop the human back off at his house."

"You aren't going without me," Noah fought.

Kalvin grinned. "No, you're just a human. You'd be an easy snack."

Noah took a couple strides towards Kalvin. "I'm the wide receiver on our football team. I have also played numerous other sports and have a 4.0 GPA. I think I can handle myself."

Kalvin made his stature imposing, and his pupils narrowed. "Prove it."

Noah tried to punch him, but Kalvin dodged. He tried multiple times, but he was never able to touch Kalvin. Feeling the touch of defeat, Noah went for one last punch, throwing all his body weight behind it.

It was a mistake.

Kalvin took hold of his wrist and flipped him onto the ground.

"Ya got spunk. But ya still can't come." Kalvin extended

his hand to help him up. "Either way, it's too dangerous for us if ya go."

Noah accepted Kalvin's help.

"Kalvin's right," I said. "It would draw way too much attention. There are countless creatures that would smell your blood and think only of a good meal."

"Then, I'll stay here. I won't go home without Greyson." Noah held strong eye contact with me.

Greyson gave him a look. "We need someone back at the house in case your parents come home early. The party stuff still hasn't been completely cleaned up. Your mom will flip if she comes home to that *and* us missing."

Noah's muscles relaxed slightly. "I assume that's where I come in, right?" Noah's tone was flat.

Greyson nodded.

"Fine. I'll go home, but if you're not back by the time Mom gets there tomorrow, I'm not covering for you for long."

Greyson's shoulders tightened and he seemed to be holding back a grin. "Sounds good." He turned back to me. "When do we leave?"

We walked Noah back to his house and started on our way to Tamara's. The two-hour hike was mostly uphill, through the forest and up the base of a mountain. Greyson stayed attentive. In fact, his hearing might have been even sharper than mine. I watched as he and Kalvin looked towards something I didn't hear. It was interesting and made me ponder all the possibilities of what he could be underneath his human skin.

Kalvin was the first one to break the silence. "So... there's one thing I haven't been able to figure out. If you've been going to school with Elisia all this time, how come ya two didn't notice that ya both had Anchors?"

Greyson and I looked at one another.

"I tried to keep mine covered. I didn't like lying all the time," I answered with a shrug.

Greyson nodded. "Noah and I figured it would cause a lot of questions since getting a tattoo before eighteen is illegal. I hid it until my birthday a couple months ago."

How interesting, being able to compare stories about hiding our Anchors. I never had anyone that understood that aspect of my life, not in the human world at least.

I suddenly realized I was staring and quickly looked away.

Again, Kalvin broke the silence. "Is Noah your brother or do ya two just live together?

Greyson scratched his head. "He's my brother but not by blood."

Greyson looked down as he walked, a sad look in his eye. He shook his head like he was trying to shake something from it. When he looked up, all sadness was gone.

"Anyway, is your mom a dragon? Cause I'm starting to wonder if I thought this through."

Kalvin snickered. "Yup. She's big. Scaly. And breathes fire." He made a gesture of monster claws and a snarl on his face.

Greyson's eyes widened, and I saw his Adam's apple bob.

I picked up a twig and threw it at Kalvin. "Hey! Don't scare him." I turned to Greyson. "Tamara's not big and scary. She's super sweet." I glared at Kalvin's mischievous grin. "Unlike her son."

Greyson laughed, but I could tell it was strained.

A snap echoed in the woods behind us.

Kalvin moved first. I grabbed Greyson's wrist, following Kalvin into the underbrush off the side of the path. We crouched as we made our way to an elderberry bush, squatting behind it, hoping the smell would mask us from whatever was coming.

The earth began to shake, footsteps vibrating the ground. Whatever it was, it was big.

I peered around the bush. Giant feet dragged a wooden cart of some sort. I leaned back to look at Kalvin. I mouthed the word *Cyclops* to him. He nodded. We needed to wait for it to pass us.

Taking a step back, Greyson lost his balance.

His legs suddenly slid out from underneath him, lifting him upside down into a tree. There he dangled about ten feet in the air.

"Kalvin, he triggered a trap," I whispered hoarsely.

I clenched my jaw as I ran to the tree Greyson was tied to. Kalvin tossed me his dagger, and I quickly cut the rope. Greyson fell to the ground with an audible thud. Kalvin helped him to his feet.

But when Greyson looked up, his face went pale. I turned around to see one large eye staring at us.

"Lunch," the cyclops said, a gruesome grin spreading on its face.

8

We ran through the forest, departing from the path to lose the cyclops who could not maneuver well in the trees. I tried to keep Greyson in my sight while also keeping track of my footing. If there was one trap, there were probably more. I didn't know what creature set the last one, and I really didn't want to find out.

A growl echoed in the distance, and the earth stopped shaking.

I think we lost him.

We stopped to catch our breaths.

Kalvin cleared his throat. "We'll take the long way. I didn't realize any ogres would be transporting goods today."

I nodded and followed him.

We avoided being loud the rest of the way as we took in the scenery. A pixie village perched high in the trees where we could not see them, but they saw us. Pixies fluttered down, their little bodies only six inches tall, covered in cute outfits and pixie dust. The gold glitter got everywhere. The pixies tried to talk to us, but I knew better. Once you talk to a pixie, they don't leave you alone.

Greyson was unaware of that.

Soon, we had a large number following us, trying to talk to Greyson. They kept asking him ridiculous questions in tiny, chipper voices. I wanted to shoo them away, yet seeing Greyson interact with them made me feel warm inside. With a Cheshire grin plastered across his face, he answered every question, even asking a few of his own.

"Who are you?"

"What's your favorite color?"

"What's pizza like? We hear it's delicious."

Our eyes met, his wide and transparent in all the excitement. I smiled back. It made me happy that his first interaction with Perfidious was a good one. There were a lot of different ways it could have gone.

Kalvin got annoyed though. "Come on, get out of here!"

The pixies gasped and scattered. Greyson waved goodbye to them and jogged to be closer to us.

"That was cool," he beamed.

"Pixies are extremely social. I'm surprised they left at all." I stepped over a root. The trees were taller there and more spread out.

"Those were pixies? I thought they were fairies." The excitement was gone from his voice.

"Nope. Pixies are the smaller ones," I explained. "Fairies are usually similar to the size of humans, just on the shorter side."

"How do you know all of this?" Greyson asked.

Kalvin laughed. "She's here often. That's how. Ya haven't been in Perfidious for very long, but there are rumors and stereotypes about every species. Stick around and you'll learn a lot just by hearing what others have to say."

Greyson seemed as though he wanted to ask more questions but wasn't sure what he wanted to say, so he remained silent.

We made it to Tamara's cave as the sun was beginning to descend from its peak. I walked into the giant entrance, marveling at the smooth floor that didn't quite match the jagged rocks above.

It had been a long time since I had visited Tamara, but it still felt like I shrunk when I entered. Tamara was a blacksmith for all kinds of weapons for many different species, including dragons and giants.

She was easily twenty feet tall.

I didn't see anyone at first. The giant space seemed empty other than a large counter that looked more like a stone storefront with a hallway behind it, leading to the back room where Tamara worked.

Human arms wrapped around me and hugged me tightly. It didn't surprise me. Tamara probably smelled me from a mile away. I hugged her and pulled back with a smile. Her dress, from a different era each time I saw her, appeared of the Renaissance fashions. Her orange eyes, more reptilian than Kalvin's, glowed warmly, but other than that, she appeared human.

At the moment anyway.

After the Human Wars, many creatures like dragons learned to shift forms so they could take the shape of humans, but it wasn't easy for them to hold the form for very long.

Her red ringlets flowed around her face as she looked at her son. "I told you so."

"You don't know why we're here," Kalvin sassed.

"The sword didn't work." She arched her eyebrow. His silence told her she was right. "I. Told. You. So."

She hugged him as he rolled his eyes.

Greyson walked in behind us and saw the woman hugging Kalvin. "I thought you said your mom was a dragon?"

Tamara looked at the new boy questioningly and smelled the air, trying to read the newcomer. Without warning, she jumped back several feet. Tamara let out a hiss, showing pointed teeth. A set of maroon scales shimmered across her body, then they disappeared as fast as they appeared. She looked human again.

Tamara looked disappointed at her son, and anger dripped from her words. "Kalvin, why did you bring him here? You know how I feel about *his* kind."

I interrupted Kalvin as I stepped forward. "Tamara, we don't know what he is." I saw her body lose some of its tension and I continued. "The Coalfell Elders assigned me to watch him. I thought by bringing him along we'd be able to teach him about Perfidious."

Tamara exhaled and seemed to calm down a little more. "Well, I know what he is. This boy is part shapeshifter." She turned to Greyson. "What's your name?"

Greyson's eyes were wide, and his voice was slightly shaky, but he stood tall as he extended a hand to Tamara. "Gr-Greyson."

Tamara walked forward and shook his hand.

"H-how—" Greyson cleared his throat. "How do you know if I'm part shapeshifter? I-I thought you were a dragon."

"I can smell it in your scent, a strange mix at that. But the smell of a shapeshifter—it's a scent I'll never forget." She didn't need to go into detail. Kalvin and I knew the reasoning behind it. "I may be a judgmental lizard, but I can be civil. Although I don't look like it at the moment, I *am* a dragon. Don't get me confused with those *other* beings. They can shift into anything while I have only evolved into being able to shift into a human form for a short while." She turned her attention back to me, the disgust vanishing from her eyes. "Why don't we find you some suitable blades, hm?"

"I thought the sword would work for weapon training." Kalvin spoke up. "But she kept complaining 'bout it being in only one hand. I could've easily taken her arm off several times."

I narrowed my eyes at Kalvin even though I knew he was right. "It's not like I'm a newbie. I know how to fight with a weapon, just not a sword."

"That's because Elisia fights with her whole being. She is smart, clever, and quick. She needs a blade that will work with that, not some bulky sword."

Goosebumps covered my arms. Tamara had never seen me fight, but that's how she was. Years of experience made it so that she could look at someone and know what kind of weapon they needed.

She walked through the massive cave, making her way into the back. Her shadow against the cave wall revealed her changed form with wings extending from her back.

She probably needed to release the human form for a minute. I don't think Tamara was used to holding it for so long.

"So, what is a shapeshifter exactly? How does it work being a shapeshifter half-breed?" Greyson asked.

I started to tell him what I knew about shapeshifters, what I had picked up around the village anyway, but Kalvin spoke over me.

"Not here. Not around my mom. She doesn't like talking about it."

I nodded to Kalvin, though I didn't fully believe him. I knew how much he missed Aaron. I missed him too.

"Later," I told Greyson.

In moments, Tamara came around the corner still in her dragon form. She shifted right before reaching us. In her hands were two blades with strange handles that pointed perpendicular to the blade instead of straight, like a sword.

I grabbed the handles eagerly. The blades sat parallel to my forearms, only a few centimeters away, extending from my hand to just past my elbows. I spun the blades around and felt their sharpness cutting through the air.

They made me feel dangerous.

"They're freshly sharpened," Tamara said, satisfied. She handed me the straps with the sheaths already in place. "Be careful when you spar with my son. It will cut through dragon skin."

"Thank you, Tamara. They're beautiful." I strapped the sheaths over my jeans and slid the blades into them with a gentle click. Tamara extended her open arms to me. I hugged her, tightly. "Alright, well, I guess we better get back before my father learns that I'm out of the village... again. See you next time."

I nodded and let Kalvin say his goodbyes.

"Thanks, Mom," Kalvin said, making Tamara's features brighten.

"You'll learn someday, Kalvin." Tamara turned her attention to Greyson, eying him up and down. A small smile pulled at the corner of her lips. "Give the long sword to Greyson. He'll be able to wield it well. You try to figure out why, and next time, we'll compare notes."

I waved to Tamara, regretting that we couldn't stay longer. It went unsaid that we had to go sooner than later. It surprised me that Greyson remained quiet. I knew he would probably have more questions later.

I glanced over at him. He was staring at Tamara, studying her as we exited the cave.

I remembered the first time I visited. I had wanted to stay the night in the cave because I felt it was unfair that Kalvin could and I couldn't. Tamara had to explain to me I was half-elf and not part-dragon. Tamara's own scent covers up the scent of the human blood in Kalvin, so no monsters would come looking for a half-breed. With my genes not containing any dragon, I would be a liability, and Tamara didn't want to risk anything happening to Kalvin or me.

Our trio reached the bottom of the mountain. The terrain shifted from rocky to soft, green grass. Hills stretched out in front of us, mostly covered in trees.

Greyson cleared his throat. "Okay, I guess I'm poking the elephant in the room, but why does Tamara hate shapeshifters so much?"

I lost my footing and almost tripped. My eyes quickly went to Kalvin. He didn't even turn around.

"A shapeshifter killed my dad." Kalvin's voice was void of emotions, but for him, it just showed how sad he really was. He didn't like talking about Aaron. "It was a while ago."

Greyson placed his hand on Kalvin's shoulder as we walked. Kalvin didn't look back as Greyson spoke. "I know the feeling. Noah's mom and my mom were inseparable, so we grew up as brothers. About eight years ago, my mom and grandmother got into a car accident..." Greyson dropped his hand as Kalvin turned around. "Neither survived. I didn't have any record of any living family members, and I guess my mom had it in her will that Noah's parents would take custody of me if anything ever happened."

I stayed silent. Greyson's honesty caught me off guard. It was a lot to admit to people who were essentially strangers.

Kalvin nodded. "Makes sense. If your mom and grandma weren't human, they'd barely have any human records to begin with, let alone any family there."

Greyson's face turned red. "Like I said, I know the feeling."

The fireflies started to appear, and beady eyes began watching us from the shadows. We made a plan for Kalvin and Greyson to continue on to the cellar while I stopped to grab some food. There was a little restaurant run by mole-like creatures. They didn't like to be around anything very noisy, so they built Shakey's outside of Coalfell, five minutes north of my root cellar.

After grabbing the food, I started towards my bunker. Rain dripped from the sky, and rumbles echoed in the distance. I sighed, quickening my pace.

I dropped down into the room and sealed the door behind me. Kalvin had already set up his normal bed on the floor and made one for Greyson near my dresser.

"What's going on?" I asked, setting the bag of food on the bed.

Kalvin responded. "We're staying here tonight. It's past dark and raining. If you go home now, you'll only get in more trouble. Text your mom and let her know you're staying here because of the weather."

I looked to Greyson. "You sure?"

Greyson shrugged. "Noah's parents shouldn't be home until sometime tomorrow. He'll be fine without me for a night. Plus, I have more questions about Perfidious."

"Okay," I said. "I got us all Shakey's special."

Kalvin whooped as I started to pull them out of the bag.

I threw Greyson the burrito-looking wrap. He eyed me suspiciously. I rolled my eyes.

"Just try it."

I handed Kalvin his wrap as Greyson unwrapped the paper and took a bite. His eyes went wide, and he quickly swallowed.

"This is really good! What's in it?"

I unwrapped my own from its package. "No one knows. It's a secret recipe. But it's one of my go-to places around Coalfell."

I looked around the room and realized that I'd probably need more blankets. With just Kalvin and me, it worked, but with another person, I definitely didn't have enough. I decided I had to grab more supplies for my cellar in town. Not the next day though.

There was something I needed to do.

9

I tiptoed out of the cellar and shut the door without making a sound. The crisp air caused the hair on my arms to stand up as I made my way to Coalfell. It only took a couple minutes to reach the outskirts of the village.

Most were still in their beds, getting another couple hours of sleep, but the ones who had businesses were wide awake. Shutters opened all over town as merchants slowly set up their shops. I scanned the various faces for one in particular.

The trees above rustled in the wind, letting in soft streams of morning sun. Warmth covered my skin as I continued my search.

I spotted pointed ears and golden hair above the thickening crowd. Gina's lean-to wasn't open for the day quite yet, but I knew she'd have what I needed.

"Daughter of Erlan, what a pleasure!" Gina spoke with glee.

I hated it when others referred to me like that.

"Morning, Gina. I need a lunch. One with extra fruit,

please." I took out my coins from my bag and extended them to her.

"Going on another journey, are we?" Her smile faltered as she handed me one of the lunches she had already prepared.

"Not exactly." I tried to act casual as I put the two boxes in my bag. "Just going to see a friend. We're meeting for a picnic, and we're supposed to bring our own food," I lied.

Her face brightened again. "Well! I hope the weather holds out." She motioned towards the sky. "It looks like it might rain some more."

I thanked her as I took the lunch and went on my way.

The trip wasn't far from what I remembered, though I didn't recall exactly where the abandoned church was located.

---

6 years before

When I first started exploring Perfidious, I got lost more than a few times. One of those times, I found an old, broken-down church. The sun was descending, and I knew that I couldn't find my way back in the dark. Nor would it be safe. After I got my campsite ready, a statue from the top of the inside wall began to move.

"May I help you?" it asked.

I jumped with a squeal, and the gargoyle leaned forward into the light. I had never met a gargoyle before. My palms were shaking, and I could feel my knees weakening.

"I was...um...exploring, but it's getting dark out, so I'm

gonna just head home." I answered him with a nervous giggle, quickly grabbing my things.

I didn't want to admit to him I was lost, nor did I want to show him that I was scared. Dad said some monsters can smell fear.

I heard a whoosh of air, and suddenly the gargoyle was blocking my exit. He shook, and the stones began to fall off until a human with wings stood in front of me. "No need to fear, little Elisia. It is especially dangerous out during dusk. Have dinner with me. Wait about an hour after the sun sets. It will be a lot safer, especially for a half-breed." He spoke with a soft, wise voice.

"How do you know my name?"

He grinned. "My name is Lexon. I work with your father. He has a picture of you in his office."

I narrowed my eyes and crossed my arms. "So, my dad sent you to find me, and you're gonna tell him I was lost?"

He widened his eyes and blinked before he roared with amusement. "You're sassy. No, I'm not going to tell your father. I don't really work for him. I work for the Council."

I sat down, relaxing a bit, and watched him pull out a packed lunch with a sandwich and fruit while he told me about his position at the castle. Lexon was in charge of knowing everything, even the smallest of things, and had been for the past few hundred years.

After we ate, he asked a Lighter Cat—a small, cat-looking creature that left a set of paw prints that glow at night—to guide me home. I was about to follow the cat, but Lexon stepped in front of me once more.

"Elisia, I will see you again."

I laughed. "You're a gargoyle. Gargoyles can't see the future."

"You are right, my dear. But I have a strong feeling about you. I come here quite often. If you ever need to know anything or need my help, all you have to do is come back to this church and yell my name."

I left the church that night, thinking I would never return. Instead, I found myself following a path I thought would lead me the right way. I knew it was the same direction as Tamara's, but instead of going up into the mountain, I needed to go around the base.

It seemed like an hour had passed, and I still couldn't see anything familiar. The trees started to get thicker, and the path began to thin. I stopped and turned around, certain I was going the wrong way.

A Lighter Cat stepped onto the path in front of me. It tilted its purple and gold head, gazing intently at my face. I didn't know what to do. Those cats were rare. I had only seen the one that led me home that night from the church.

It blinked a couple of times, and then sprinted off the path through a bush. The cat's small body barely made a sound. I shook my head and went to walk away but hesitated. My gut told me to follow it.

I glanced in the direction the cat had disappeared.

What did I have to lose? Well, besides my life.

I maneuvered through the thick underbrush, ignoring the briars that clung to my jeans. I stuck my hand through the next bush to find no resistance and struggled through, only to be rewarded with the sight of church ruins.

Parts of the church still stood tall, but most of it had crumbled away with age. At one point, it was probably the size of a three-story building. Remnants of a tower came out of the far corner. Stairs twisted up with no walls and nowhere to go. Stained glass stuck out like teeth from the windows, leaving their stories in shatters.

Inside, there was a ledge that might have either been the floor to the second story or a balcony. I looked around the walkway, curious to see if Lexon was sitting on the edge like he was before. No stone resembled a gargoyle.

I yelled his name at the top of my lungs. There was no reply. I sat on the steps in front of the small stage and ate some of the food I brought while I waited.

It seemed like forever. The sun beat down, causing me to sweat, with only a few clouds for relief. Perhaps it would not rain, despite Gina's prediction.

A shadow blocked the sun's view and stopped my train of thought.

Stone wings descended. He collided with the ground, sounding as though he'd broken through the floor, but he didn't leave a dent in the old rubble. I watched as he shook the stone from his shoulders, the pieces disappearing before they hit the ground.

Lexon smiled as he straightened. He was in his human form with giant stone wings. His black hair was longer, and he also had a goatee.

"Hello, little Elisia. It's nice to see you again." He walked up to me and hugged me, as though I was an old friend.

"It's good to see you too, Lexon."

"What have you been up to?" He asked politely, letting go of me.

I glared at him, slightly startled by the question. "Don't you already know?"

Lexon sat down on one of the broken pews. "Amuse me."

I paced as I explained. "Well, I found out one of my friends, who I *thought* was human, is actually a half-breed. When I took him to the Elders, they assigned me to watch him and one of his friends who stupidly refuses to leave his side."

Lexon spoke during my short pause. "Greyson and Noah. I hear that Greyson could be a being of three?"

I stopped pacing and frowned, not recognizing the phrase. "What's a being of three?"

"It is similar to a half-breed, like you and I, but instead has two different species of monster running through his human veins."

"Hmm." I dove into a train of thought, trying to figure out what that would mean for Greyson.

"You may continue, little Elisia." Lexon's smile was encouraging, but his eyes told me I wasn't telling him anything new.

"Well, we went to see Tamara, and she said that Greyson smelled strange. But she also said that he was definitely part shapeshifter."

Lexon arched an eyebrow. "So, why exactly are you here?"

"I heard the rumors about a shapeshifter near Gross Peak. It's the only one I have heard of since they killed King Lawrence. Do you know his exact location?"

Lexon frowned and looked unsure. "This shapeshifter you speak of is not of the friendly sorts."

From the stories I'd heard, it didn't surprise me. Lexon must have seen the look on my face.

"But you already know this, little Elisia. Convince me it

is a good idea to tell you. Why do you want to know?" The look in his eyes told me he already had his answer, but I couldn't tell what it was.

"The Elders gave him no answers. Tamara gave him more answers than they did. I just want to help him know where he is from," I confessed, but he was still frowning.

My eyes widened as a mental light bulb clicked on in my head. I realized it wasn't the full truth. I continued talking more to myself than to Lexon.

"I also want him to learn what his abilities are and learn how to control them, so he doesn't accidentally hurt anyone or...get himself killed." An image of the Mourning Willow, of all the murdered half-breeds, flashed through my head.

Without saying a word or changing his expression, Lexon pulled out a piece of parchment and began to draw. Silence filled the room for a few minutes before he finally put away his pen. He looked up at me as he handed me his work.

It was a map, complete with landmarks to show me where to turn. It was the best set of drawn directions I had ever seen.

"Be careful, little Elisia. This is a dangerous path you are turning down, but your reasons are noble. I wish you luck." He looked down at the blades sheathed at my sides and studied me for a second. "I guess you've grown some since we last met. If you find out anything *interesting* on your way. You will let me know, won't you?"

I nodded. His wings spread out and stone returned to his form. He flew away without looking back. I couldn't help feeling that he wasn't telling me everything.

I made my way back to my root cellar as fast as I could.

It was evening by the time I returned. I walked up to see Kalvin and Greyson sitting near the entrance.

A twig snapped under my foot. Kalvin got up from his seat abruptly. He turned around and stomped to me, his expression tight.

"Where the hell were ya?" He cut me off before I could answer. His fists clenched at his sides, and his eyes seemed more orange than normal. "I woke up this morning to find ya *missing*. We didn't hear ya leave. It looked like ya just disappeared! Do you know how worried I was? Next time you run off, tell someone before you go. Or, I don't know," he threw his arms into the air, "don't go alone! The only reason I'm not breathing fire right now is because I ran into Gina, and she mentioned seeing ya this morning."

My face fell. I didn't mean to make him mad. Or worry him.

"I had to go see someone that knew where the shapeshifter near Gross Peak lives. So, tomorrow, after I get supplies, I'm taking Greyson to see it." My voice was soft as I explained.

But I didn't regret going, and he knew it.

His shoulders tightened, then loosened just as fast. He turned around and started stomping away. "I'll be back. You're not goin', Elisia. You're goin' home! And if ya don't go home, I'm telling your dad."

I sighed and yelled to him as he walked away. "Where are you going?"

"I said I'll be back!" he yelled, not turning around.

"Stubborn jerk," I mumbled.

He was probably right. I knew better than to go on my own, but it wasn't like I went far or into monster territory.

Plus, I could take care of myself. I didn't know what he was so worried about.

I turned to Greyson, his gaze full of pain. Guilt stirred inside me. "I met with a gargoyle that knows where a shapeshifter lives. He gave me a map. I thought you might want to learn how to use your abilities."

I pulled the map out of my bag.

Greyson's muscles were tight. He barely glanced at the map before he looked up at me from his seat, giving me a tight smile.

"Thanks, Elisia." He paused before continuing. "You should have told us where you were going. Kalvin was really worried." His eyebrows drew together, and he exhaled forcefully. "I was worried too. You shouldn't have done that."

He turned his head so I couldn't see his face.

"I know," I admitted. I took a couple steps toward him and put myself right in his gaze, making him look at me. My next words were soft, hoping to inspire forgiveness. "I was just trying to help. If I told Kalvin I was going to see the gargoyle, he would have never let me go alone. I thought the gargoyle would only come if I was alone."

Greyson nodded slowly. "So, this shapeshifter, is he— or she—dangerous?"

"Probably," I answered. "But we'd all go. It'd be stupid to go alone...if Kalvin will even come. Shapeshifters are some of the strongest monsters I know of. From what I've heard, they can turn into any animal, person, or creature with one touch. Even if it is just a handshake, a pureblood shapeshifter could copy the whole being."

"Hm," Greyson said. "I have to head home before Noah's mom freaks out. We'll talk about it tomorrow."

That was the end of the conversation.

I took Greyson home, but he barely spoke as we walked. Guilt kept me quiet as I bit my lip, unsure what I should say. Greyson thanked me for showing him the way home and went inside.

The dirt road was the fastest way back to my house. Only dark windows welcomed me. I walked in the front door and noticed a glow coming from the living room. Mom was asleep in the recliner with the TV on. I grabbed a blanket to cover her as she stirred awake.

She mumbled something.

"Sorry, I'm home so late. I'll see you in the morning," I whispered.

She groaned and relaxed into the chair again.

I made my way to my bed, changing into pajamas along the way. Bright red numbers glowed in the darkness, 11:34. I crawled under the covers and laid down to sleep.

But sleep didn't come.

I couldn't stop thinking of Kalvin. He left so upset. I didn't know if he would be back or when I would see him again. We'd fought before, of course. Usually one of us just needed time to cool down before we talked rationally. Who knew how long that might be.

It felt like I was laying there for hours without sleep. I laid still with my eyes closed, facing the wall, listening to the chirping of crickets outside my open window.

Suddenly, the noise quieted.

A small breeze caressed my cheek, and someone sat on the side of my bed.

Kalvin.

I pretended to be asleep, too tired to fight with him.

"I know you're awake." Kalvin whispered. He softly laid

down next to me, wrapping his arm gently around my stomach. He took a deep breath before continuing. "All ya need to do is listen. I'm sorry for the way I acted. I don't know what I'd do without ya...Just the thought of losing ya," I could feel him shake at the thought. "It scares the hell outta me. If you were really worried about the gargoyle not showing up, then tell me. I would've understood. I know that you can take care of yourself. Please don't just disappear without a word again. Ya can't do that to me. Besides my mom, you're all I have left."

He tightened his arm around me and stayed for a while, body heat radiating through the blankets. I placed my hand on top of his arm. The sound of his pulse quickening filled my ears while the familiar scent of campfire and pine wood surrounded me. Kalvin's presence calmed the storm thundering around my head. Confident that we'd be all right, I drifted off to sleep.

10

My eyes opened just slightly to the blinding sun peeking through my shades. I turned over to find the window shut and Kalvin gone. That dummy. My legs swung unwillingly off the bed as I forced myself to sit. A person passed by my door, but I was too slow to see who it was. I looked back to the window and stretched. My muscles tightened and released, a couple joints popping pleasantly in the process.

"Oh. You are awake." Mom stood in my doorway, a half-eaten bagel in her hand. "I thought I saw you stirring. Want anything special for breakfast?"

I shook my head, still unable to process how to speak.

"Coffee?" Mom offered, and my eyes widened as I nodded my head vigorously.

She vanished from the door only to appear seconds later. The hot cup warmed my hands instantly as I took a sip. My insides came alive with heat as the coffee made its way to my stomach.

Mmm.

I brought the cup to my lips again, taking several long gulps of the life juice.

Mom laughed as she made her way toward the door. "I'll be leaving in a little bit to run some errands. There is a chores list on the fridge. I expect all of it to be done by the time your father gets home. Understood?"

I nodded as she left.

I grabbed my phone off my nightstand. Two missed calls from Greyson. I dialed his number and waited for him to pick up.

I didn't have to wait long.

"Hey, Elisia. What's up?" Greyson's cheerful grin could be heard through the phone.

"Why did you call me so early?" I asked him as I got up to pick out clothes.

"We need to talk about going to see the shapeshifter," he demanded.

"Are you sure about this?"

"I know Kalvin said we weren't going, but we have to. It's the only way I'm going to learn about what I am. I called Noah's parents, and they haven't told me anything, even though they're acting like they know something. They just keep saying we'll talk about it when they get home." Unease set into his voice.

I thought about it for a second. Kalvin and I weren't fighting anymore, so he would probably be willing to come with us. I certainly didn't want to go without him.

"Elisia?" Greyson pleaded on the phone.

"Fine," I finally answered. "Pack a bag for the day. Bring food and water. We just have to make sure we're back before it gets too late. My parents won't be happy if I'm not home tonight. We'll also have to go pick up Kalvin."

"Okay! We'll be there soon." Greyson hung up.

I didn't like the way he said *we*.

I grabbed a backpack and filled it with some food, water, matches and a first aid kit. I reached under my bed and grabbed my blades.

I really hoped he didn't mean that he was bringing Noah.

I waited on the front porch for Greyson. Muffled voices echoed down the road, confirming my fears. Once Greyson came into view, I saw Noah with him. They both had on backpacks and hiking clothes. I sighed and brought my hand through my hair, trying to think of a way to convince them it was a bad idea.

I got up and crossed my arms. "He's not coming," I yelled down the road so they could hear.

"Ha. I am definitely coming, right, Greyson?" Noah walked tall, his head high.

I snapped my head to Greyson and raised my eyebrows.

Greyson shrugged. "He's coming. Which way to Kalvin's house?" He started to walk around my house towards the woods.

I caught up with him and whispered, "Do you realize how dangerous this is?" I looked back to see Noah's wide grin. "His scent could attract a lot of monsters our way. The kind of attention we don't want."

Greyson kept walking. "We're not changing our minds."

I shook my head and led them to Kalvin's house. Their determination struck me silent. I didn't know how to handle that kind of stubbornness. Maybe Kalvin could talk some sense into them.

We walked up to his house, and I knocked on the door. It took Kalvin a couple minutes before he answered.

His eyes were half open as he glared at me, and he was only wearing sweatpants, no shirt. I had to pull my eyes away from his muscled chest and defined abs.

"You want to go this early?" Kalvin asked. He rubbed his eyes and looked at the two boys with me. "Why is the human here?"

I felt bad waking him up since I had no idea what time he actually left my house the night before. The idea of him next to me invaded my mind. Heat rose to my cheeks.

"Um, Greyson wouldn't back down," I said, biting my lip. My mind needed to get back on track.

I saw the corner of Kalvin's lips pull up.

"And yes," I shifted my weight and looked away from him. "We're all ready to leave. I'd really like it if you came with us."

I turned back to face Kalvin, only for him to shut the door.

I knocked several times, growing louder with each knock. "Kalvin! You're not being fair. Open up! Let's talk about this."

When Kalvin finally opened the door, his clothes were changed, and he was fastening a backpack on his shoulders.

"You're loud in the morning." He walked past me, pausing to whisper in my ear, "Ya also kick in your sleep."

I felt my face flush. He turned around and laughed

wholeheartedly. It made me smile because I knew that we were even.

We started on our way to Gross Peak. I took the lead because I had Lexon's map. Greyson was behind me and Noah was in front of Kalvin, a classic defensive position to have the two weakest fighters in the middle. That way if anything approached us from any side, Kalvin or I could take care of it.

I scanned our surroundings. The trees and plants were the same as any other forest. If we didn't see any monsters, I could easily pretend we were on a normal walk in a normal forest.

I turned to see Noah taking in his surroundings as we came up to a tight curl of a river. His eyes widened as he saw the majestic blue, purple, and green fins peeking out of the water.

"That's the Chelan River. Its name means 'deep water'. No one really knows how deep it goes, except for maybe the mermaids or nymphs," I informed them.

His eyes sparked, and he sent a sly smirk to Greyson. "This would be an awesome place to throw a party, right?"

"Ha!" Kalvin sarcastically sneered. "Go ahead, get yourself killed."

I rolled my eyes and went back to tracking our route. Lexon had instructed us to follow the curve near the river, then to follow the moss to the north.

"You think everywhere is a good place to have a party." Greyson cracked up.

"Right, but that's why I'll be the best event planner in the country. I know everything there is to know about throwing a party anywhere."

I turned my head so they could hear me. "Well, I wouldn't throw a party here—"

Noah didn't let me finish. "Yeah, yeah. *Too dangerous*, right?" He sarcastically shivered like he was scared before he looked away from me.

"That and humans aren't supposed to know about Perfidious, right?" Greyson added.

Kalvin chimed in. "Exactly, so don't try to bring any other humans here."

I didn't know what Noah's problem was, but there was definitely something wrong. Did he not like me? I always thought that Noah was a smart, happy guy. However, since I started talking to him about Perfidious, he'd seemed almost angry with me. I wanted to ask him about it. I deserved to know why he was acting like that.

After all, he was the one that talked me into telling Greyson everything. Greyson was at least listening to Kalvin and me. The rules, the dangers, and the cool stuff. He took it all seriously. Noah, on the other hand, kept acting like it was all a joke.

My blood was boiling. I glared at Noah, who was still having a verbal battle with Kalvin about humans in Perfidious.

I took an aggressive step forward.

A hand gently pulled on my wrist.

Greyson smiled softly at me. His eyes stared into mine but seemed to be looking beyond the surface. He glanced at Noah, and then back to me.

"He just needs time. He's not used to change," he whispered.

I nodded. *How did he know what I was thinking?*

I looked away from him and focused on a tree ahead.

That look in his eyes...I had to look away. It seemed like he was looking into my head, not just into my eyes.

The tree swayed unnaturally.

None of the trees around it were moving, but that one tree looked like it was getting tossed around by a storm.

"Kalvin?" I asked.

He stopped talking and looked at me.

"Is that what I think it is?" I pointed in front of us.

Kalvin stopped walking and went pale. "I hate those damn birds."

As though they heard him, a flock of thunderbirds flew from the trees. I could see little sparks of electricity ignite underneath their wings, thunder clapping with each stroke.

"Run!" Kalvin yelled at Greyson and Noah.

The thunderbirds caught up to us. Their beaks shocked us as they pecked at our heads and arms. The little bolts of energy caused my muscles to twitch, but I pushed through.

Noah wasn't doing so well. More birds swarmed around him, and he was starting to slow down. I swatted at the birds, trying to get some of them off him.

Kalvin waved at us. "This way!"

He pushed to run faster, grabbing a branch and pulling it back.

"Down!" I shouted.

Noah and Greyson followed my lead and dropped to the ground, but the birds didn't understand what was about to happen. They stayed in the air, hovering as Kalvin let go of the branch.

The branch hit them as though it were a bat hitting a home run.

I got up and jogged over to Kalvin, breathing hard, Greyson and Noah on my heels.

"Should I tell you 'I told you so' now or later?" I asked Noah.

He narrowed his eyes at me but looked too out of breath to respond.

Decades passed, and the Shapeshifter King rallied as many monsters as he could find. He appointed scouts to spread the word of their new home, a safe haven for monsters. By 1453, Perfidious—a combination of vast flatlands, deep valleys, and steeply sloped mountains—seemed to occupy the remainder of the monsters, but the Shapeshifter King was saddened by the low numbers that had endured the Human War.

However, not all was right on the borders of Perfidious. News spread of the monsters being there, and humans gathered to try to catch one escaping. The Shapeshifter King devised a solution. He called on the druids to create a barrier to separate the outside world and Perfidious. The druids did as they were asked, leaving only seven small pockets, or gates, around the area where anyone could enter or leave. Connecting the gates was an impenetrable wall of foliage.

The Shapeshifter King built his own castle in the middle of Perfidious. The remaining monsters set up villages and homes scattered throughout, mostly staying among their own species.

The Shapeshifter King, quickly realizing that Perfidious was not the perfect sanctuary he had intended, knew he'd have many hardships to overcome.

An excerpt from The King's Legacy:
A Complete History of Perfidious

11

Before heading up to the cliff, we made a deal to meet at the bottom if something attacked us again. It was an open area, the crossroads of many paths.

The view over the cliffs seemed like a sea of fog. Tree tips swung in the breeze, but nothing could be seen below. With no way of telling how far up we were, I studied the twists and turns on the map, trying to ignore the bad feeling growing in my gut. The map said it was about five more miles, which meant another hour and a half approximately.

Everyone mostly snacked on the way there, but I focused on the map. Traveling in monster territory wasn't the safest task, and I wanted to make sure we didn't get lost. That was the last thing we needed.

The drawing of the cave did nothing to prepare me for the real thing.

I put the map away and stared into the black depths of a hole in the side of the mountain. The cave seemed much smaller than Tamara's but was much more intimidating. We stood at the entrance, no one making a move to go inside.

"We're supposed to go in there, right?" Noah asked, his eyes never leaving the cave.

I nodded. "Let's go. Stay close together."

I barely made out a hidden crack in the stone a couple feet into the cave, large enough for something my size to fit into. The darkness obscured other fissures deeper inside, and I couldn't make out if they were real passages or just indents in the cave wall. If any creature had wandered in there for shelter, they'd have no way of seeing an attack coming.

And I was worried that would happen to us.

Greyson and Noah scanned the cave. Kalvin seemed to hold his breath. He looked over at me. Our eyes met, and he nodded. It was definitely the shapeshifter's hideout.

I inhaled, ready to call out to see if anything would answer.

A sound echoed in the cave before I could, the sound of something slithering on the walls. I immediately turned around to find what looked like a crocodile but more human-like.

Kalvin produced a large dagger from his bag.

"You come into my home and threaten me." The shapeshifter sounded like a snake speaking human words. "What do you want?"

I refused all instinct to grab my weapons as I stepped forward. "We are here to ask you if you could help a half-breed. He is part shapeshifter and has no idea how to use his abilities."

"Why would I help you?" The shapeshifter inhaled loudly. "He ha*ss* no blood of mine."

"He's part of your kind. I thought shapeshifters, if nothing else, didn't want their species to become a forgotten memory." Anger spilled into my words as I swallowed my fear.

I couldn't show weakness in front of the monster.

The creature's eyes widened. He grew a few inches and slithered forward. "Watch your tongue, little elf." The shapeshifter towered over me but then paused.

My left hand was clutching my weapon by instinct, and I didn't let go.

Someone cleared their throat.

"I just want to know how it works to shift." Greyson walked up next to me. His voice seemed stable, but his muscles shook. "Then, we'll leave."

The shapeshifter looked over at Greyson and relaxed slightly. "Whatever monster you come in contact with, you can turn into. Think about what you want to change, and it will appear. It'*ss* that *ss*imple."

"Can he only change into one being, or can he change different parts of himself, like what you seem to be doing?" I questioned.

The shapeshifter's head snapped to me. His eyes narrowed.

I held my breath so he wouldn't see my body tremble.

"A half-breed can probably only *ss*hift part*ss*. I like your gut*ss*. But if you come back here, I will *ss*ee if they taste a*s* good a*s* they *ss*mell. Lucky for you, I already ate." The shapeshifter licked his lips. He turned and started to walk deeper into the cave.

I relaxed a little and turned to face my friends.

Greyson grinned from ear to ear as he and Noah walked out of the cave together, talking about what Greyson could try to change into first. Kalvin kept his eyes on the monster behind us.

I motioned to him that we should leave.

A gust of wind blew past all four of us and into the cave.

Kalvin sniffed the air, turning pale. "I know what Greyson is."

A loud growl thundered behind us.

"You tricked me into helping the Impure King'*ss* *ss*pawn!"

I turned around to see the shapeshifter transforming, growing into something terrifying. Horns grew from his head, and his scaly skin turned into muscular bunches of fur.

Kalvin didn't ask questions. He grabbed my arm and pulled, wanting me to run. He let go at the mouth of the cave, and I ran as fast as I could, pushing Greyson and Noah to do the same.

My eyes widened. The shapeshifter was gaining on us. I looked back to see Noah struggling to keep up. Kalvin rolled his eyes and went back to help Noah.

The roar erupted again.

I didn't think about my next action. All I knew was that I had to do something. I grabbed Greyson's hand and pulled him a different way than Kalvin and Noah.

The shapeshifter followed us.

Kalvin noticed and yelled my name, but I couldn't stop, and I didn't look back. I pushed Greyson to run faster. I kept my mind focused on getting him out of there, out of danger and away from the beast.

The vibrations from the shapeshifter grew stronger, and I increased my speed, not even questioning how fast Greyson could run. I glanced at him next to me, startled to find that Greyson was keeping up with me running at full speed.

I turned my attention back to where I was going but only saw clouds.

It was too late to stop.

We were running too fast, and my feet ran out of solid ground. I responded immediately. My body twisted, allowing me to grab the ledge with little effort. The hard part was catching Greyson, who reached for my hand. I was so close to falling that I could only grab his fingers.

He grabbed my arm, smashing hard into the wall. Greyson's full weight yanked on my joints. It felt like someone was trying to rip off my arms.

I heard a snarl above us.

I looked up and saw its yellow eyes. The shapeshifter had grown at least two stories tall, a mangled monster that loomed over us. It was a combination of beings—giant, dragon, and minotaur—and I had seen nothing so deadly or so terrifying in my life.

"Did you think *I* wouldn't notisse the sstench of fairy?" The monster spat down at me in a deep voice. "The King'ss Legassy cannot return!"

The creature snarled as he raised his leg, and he brought it down on the hand holding us to the ledge. Pain erupted, and I could no longer hold on. We started to plummet towards the fog. I had to let go of Greyson's hand to cradle my own.

Greyson screamed.

We were going to die.

Unless...

"Greyson," I yelled, trying to ignore the pain. "Greyson!" I shouted louder.

He finally stopped screaming to look at me, his eyes watering from the wind just as mine were.

"Think about it! Think about Tamara's wings!"

He looked confused. "What?"

"Tamara's wings!" I repeated. My eyes widened as the fog started to thin. "Think about them on your back! Tamara said it extends from her shoulder blades. Turn your shoulder blades into wings!"

With a nod, he closed his eyes tightly. Suddenly, he relaxed, and a pair of red wings spread straight out from his back. He stopped falling and started gliding. Greyson opened his eyes and reached for my hand, but he was too far.

I exited the layer of fog, only to see about forty feet before I hit the trees.

"Greyson!" My voice broke into a scream.

I tensed and blocked my face against the impending collision with the branches.

A pair of arms slid around my waist. We reduced speed but were still falling. Twigs sliced into my arms as we crashed through them.

I turned my head to see Greyson concentrating hard, aiming for a small space between two trees. His wings lifted and slowed us further, but we were still going too fast. As his feet touched the ground, it felt like he tripped. He threw me, and we both tumbled a few feet before stopping in the dirt.

I closed my eyes. Sleep threatened to consume my mind, but I didn't let it. I tried to stay awake as I laid there, listening to the high pitch ringing in my ears.

I was too weak to move, my heart convulsing like a drum roll.

12

I heard a groan come from Greyson over the diminishing ringing in my ears. I tried to move and immediately regretted it. My body felt like weights had replaced my muscles.

I tried again.

I needed to see if Greyson was okay.

He had landed behind me, and I couldn't see him. My muscles screamed at me as I moved onto my elbows, pausing to take a couple deep breaths. I groaned, watching the bruises start to change the pigment of my hand and elbows. Dirt fell off me as I leaned forward to look around.

I couldn't hear Greyson moving. What if he was really hurt? What if he was unconscious?

More rustling came from behind me.

Greyson coughed and cleared his throat. "Elisia?"

I ignored the pain and turned on my side. He crawled towards me, his wings draping over his sides, dragging in the dirt. I cleared my throat to talk, but my voice was still hoarse.

"You should..." I coughed. "You should put the wings away."

His lip pulled up into a half smile as he closed his eyes tightly. The wings slowly retracted into his back. Once they were completely gone, he moved closer and sat near me, leaning his back against a tree.

My eyes searched him.

He was definitely bruised. A small cut on his cheek dripped blood but didn't look deep. My heart rate started to return to normal.

He was okay.

I let my body fall back onto the dirt to relax and heal.

After some time, I sat up and put some pressure on my left palm without thinking. Burning pain shot through my hand and wrist. I winced, cradling my hand to my chest. I couldn't bend my fingers.

"Elisia?" Greyson asked.

I quickly pulled my hand out of his sight. I didn't want him to know it was broken.

"You okay?" he continued. "I didn't hurt you in the landing, did I?"

I shook my head and hoped the pain wasn't showing on my face. "Nope, all good." Standing up, I looked at Greyson who was still sitting against the tree. "Greyson, you flew! You grew wings and saved us!"

His eyes widened as he attempted to look at his back. He felt his shirt and found giant slits cut through the cloth. His smile was huge as he attempted to jump up. "I can fly? I can fly!"

While Greyson continued to talk and repeat that he could fly, I searched for our backpacks along the path in the dirt where we tried to land. Most of the underbrush was uprooted. My bag wasn't too far from where we first touched down, but Greyson's pack was nowhere to be seen. I picked up my bag to find it squished yet still intact.

Greyson was still rambling.

I interrupted him. "We need to take some time to heal, and then we need to meet Noah and Kalvin before it gets dark."

I studied the sky. The blues started to darken to the east. The sun would set soon. It wouldn't give us enough time to get back to the village before dusk.

I returned my gaze to Greyson.

"Shouldn't we leave now? What if the shapeshifter comes after us?" Greyson asked, looking up at the cliff we fell from.

I shook my head. "We both need to rest and heal. That requires food and water."

Greyson didn't look convinced.

"I just need ten to twenty minutes to rest. I don't think I could make the hike right now to get to the meeting spot."

Greyson's eyes scanned my body. I made sure to keep my broken hand behind me. He parted his lips but didn't speak. He only nodded.

"Go search for your backpack. It probably broke off when you opened your wings. I'll get some food and water out of my pack for us."

Greyson nodded again.

I waited until he was far enough away to examine my hand. It was throbbing. Bad. It was all I could think about. There weren't any bones sticking through the skin, but I'd have to see a nurse. It would probably take weeks to heal, even with my enhanced healing.

The first aid kit held several small packages of ibuprofen. I took two, hoping the pain would start to dissipate, even just a little.

It didn't.

Grabbing some granola bars and crushed toaster pastries from my bag, I tried to push the pain from my mind. My eyes scanned for Greyson absentmindedly, but he was nowhere in sight. He hadn't been gone for very long; maybe he was still looking for his bag. Or maybe something got him. He wasn't very knowledgeable about Perfidious.

I'll just check on him.

A cool breeze descended from above. Confused, I looked up to find Greyson at the top of the trees, trying to figure out how to fly. By the looks of it, he hadn't noticed me.

Smiling, I grabbed a low hanging branch and slowly climbed up the tree one-handed. I made it close enough to his level and leaned against the tree like I'd been there for a while. Whatever he was doing, it was nowhere near graceful, and I wasn't sure it could be called flying, but he was at least staying in the air.

"You're getting better at that," I casually called to him.

He spun around and almost hit himself in the face with one of his wings. I tried not to giggle.

His cheeks flushed. "How long have you been there?"

"Not long." I shrugged.

"I couldn't find my backpack," Greyson said.

"Come on. We should eat before we have to hit the road." I started to climb down.

"Want a lift?" He offered me his hand as I reached for another branch.

"No need." Once I was about ten feet from the ground, I jumped and landed perfectly on my feet.

"Oh yeah, I forgot—you're not human," Greyson stated as his feet collided with the ground.

I laughed as he steadied himself. He closed his eyes tightly. It took a minute, but the wings eventually retracted.

"And you're part shapeshifter and part fairy, apparently," I said without thinking.

Greyson spun around a couple times, examining his shirt. "I think I'll also have to invest in some new shirts."

"There is a shop in Coalfell that sells clothing. We can get you a shirt that has wing slits."

"Really? They make those?"

I nodded.

"Sounds good." Greyson lowered his head and spoke more to himself than to me. "But I'll have to leave them somewhere Noah's parents won't find it. It's not something I can just casually wear."

He was starting to understand what it meant to hide everything he was from the people around him. Greyson's life had been normal until I saw his Anchor, while mine had been divided since I was born. I was a little envious of him. He got to live a normal life, even if it was only for a little while.

"Mhm," I replied, stuck on my train of thought. I shook my head. "I mean, you could probably keep them at my cellar if you wanted."

Greyson lifted the corner of his lips but quickly turned away.

We ate our food and drank a bottle of water each. It worried me a bit that Greyson remained silent, but I tried to keep my mind busy as we ate our food. I kept looking to the sky. Clouds had started to creep in, making it seem later than it was. We needed to get to the meeting spot before it got any later.

I checked Greyson for injuries after we picked up the stuff from dinner. His injuries had already begun to heal. The cut on his face was barely bleeding and would probably be healed by the time he got home. I leaned back to see if there were any injuries on his back, but all I saw were defined muscles, probably from all the time in football practice.

My gaze returned to his face. Greyson's expression was tight, and his eyes were narrow as he looked off into the distance.

"You okay there? If you think too much, your brain might explode."

His features softened at my joke, but he didn't respond immediately. I waited patiently as I repacked my bag.

"Do you know what the King's Legacy is?" he asked.

I paused. *He shouldn't be thinking about that.*

But to him I said, "Yeah, what about it?"

"What is it?" He still hadn't looked at me, staring at nothing with the same expression.

I explained the best I could. "It's this story about the last great king that ruled over Perfidious, King Lawrence, and his bloodline. He was a shapeshifter, and according to the history books, a great, fair leader. But the monsters didn't like that he married a fairy. They thought their king had become tainted. A group of purebloods attacked the castle one night and killed him for it."

Greyson straightened and looked down at his lap.

I continued. "His pregnant wife escaped, but no one really knows if she survived or not."

Greyson wasn't looking directly at me. He was just sitting on the ground, and I couldn't tell what he was feeling. Nervously, I fidgeted, picking the dirt out of my nails. The idea that he might be the king's descended heir was too good to be true, but I was also worried about how he would take the information.

"So, the king was a shapeshifter, and the queen was a fairy?" His monotone words told me exactly what he was thinking.

"Yes."

"And according to the shapeshifter we just met, I'm part shapeshifter and part fairy." Greyson's sparkling eyes met mine.

"It looks that way."

He said nothing.

I looked up to the sky. More clouds crowded over to make the blues barely visible. "We should start walking before it gets too late."

He nodded but still didn't speak.

"Are you okay, Greyson?"

He remained silent for a few minutes. "Since I'm part shapeshifter, part human, and now know that I'm also part fairy, tell me honestly, how likely it is that I'm part of that king's bloodline?"

"It could be likely that you are a descendent of him, but there's no way to know for sure." I placed my hand on his shoulder so he would look at me. "I also wouldn't go around telling others that you could be the king's heir. It's not safe."

His eyebrows raised as he gave me a sidelong glance. "So, the king's heir is a bad thing?"

I shook my head. "Not at all. The king's heir is something for which half-breeds have been hoping for as long as I can remember. To us, the king's heir or any descendent means a difference in the way we live. We wouldn't have to be in constant fear. But if the purebloods found out there was the slightest chance, you'd be a target."

He quickened his pace so he could stand in front of me and face me. "What would you do?"

I shook my head, unsure how to respond. "What do you mean?"

Greyson searched my eyes. "If you were in my shoes and taking on the title as the king's heir would mean you could help people you cared about, would you do it?"

I backed away from him, nervous about the question. Perfidious wasn't something I wanted for Greyson in the first place because of the danger it held for half-breeds. For him to declare himself as the king's heir, it would put a definite target on his back. He could not make a hasty mistake.

"Whoa. Slow down." I put my hands up. "No one said you were even related to the king. No one even knows if the queen survived or if her baby lived to produce a lineage. There's no need for you to put that kind of stress on your shoulders." I stared into his eyes, trying to read his thoughts.

Greyson had proven to be unpredictable.

"Okay. Then, hypothetically, say I'm the king's descendent. What should I do?"

I put up my hands in surrender. "No. That's not—"

"Elisia, I don't know what to think about this. Any of

this. Thursday, I was...I *thought* I was normal. Now, I can grow wings." He paused and took a deep breath. "And I might be the last descendent of the king. Then, there are all these expectations that go along with it. I need some advice. I'm not sure of my own thoughts right now."

His outburst made him freeze. He looked around us, probably to make sure no one else heard him, then lowered his eyes to the ground. It seemed like he had more to say but wasn't going to say it.

"Don't decide anything yet," I said softly.

He looked up at me.

"If this was happening to me," I continued, "I'd see if there was any proof. Nothing needs to be decided right now."

Greyson raised his eyebrows at the thought. I saw something change in his eyes before he turned around and continued walking.

"It's just..." Greyson said without looking at me, "if I am the king's heir, I'll have a family tree, a heritage. I would know where I came from."

I reached out and brushed my hand against his arms. He looked back at me, his eyes full of trust. "Don't think about it too much, okay?"

He nodded.

Slowly, the tension released in Greyson's shoulders.

"Wanna know something?" he asked, nudging me. "I'm glad I turned out to be part monster."

I almost lost my footing and scrunched up my nose. "Why?"

He laughed and scratched the back of his head. "Well, for starters, it gave me an excuse to get to know you. You were always by yourself at school—I guess I understand why now—but it made me wonder what kind of girl *wants* to be by herself. Now, I know it's because she's the strangest girl in the school."

My jaw dropped open, and I elbowed him in the gut.

"In the best way possible?" He shrugged his shoulders, but there was still a grin on his face.

We chatted about nothing for a while, just things that seemed insignificant given the circumstances like school and football.

It was the only way I could think of to help him.

13

Noah and Kalvin waited for us on the trail at the crossroads like we had discussed. Greyson asked me to pull Kalvin aside so he could talk to Noah privately. I assumed it was about him thinking he was the king's heir.

I grabbed Kalvin's arm and didn't say a word until we were far enough away that Greyson and Noah couldn't hear, but Kalvin still could.

Kalvin looked like he wanted to say something, but I stopped walking and interrupted him. "Listen to them."

I crossed my arms as he tuned into their conversation. His eyes widened a little. I nodded.

Kalvin shrugged. "I kinda put the pieces together back in the cave. The entire place smelled like the shapeshifter. It was easy to pick out the fairy in his scent. Think he will be strong enough to overthrow the Council?" Kalvin asked, acting more serious than I had seen him in a while.

"If he even is the heir, but this is all up to him. He's smart and picks up things quickly. Just look at how fast he ran from that shapeshifter. He had to have transformed the muscles in his legs to match my speed. Otherwise, we wouldn't have gotten away. He might just be that fast, but I think it was more than that."

"Okay. What do we do now? The king's heir is what we need to change Perfidious, and actually make it safe..." He trailed off as Greyson and Noah began to walk towards us.

"Nothing. Not until we know for sure," I answered quietly.

Kalvin nodded as he looked over to the guys, who were taking their time. "Come on, slowpokes."

He softly grabbed my left forearm with a reassuring squeeze. He then slid his hand down as he let go, grazing my broken hand. It hurt like hell, and I made a small yelping noise. Kalvin looked back, his worried eyes meeting mine. I knew I couldn't hide the pain from him.

His eyes trailed down to my hand.

"The hell? What happened?" he asked, bringing me into a section of moonlight to get a better view.

The base of my fingers, my knuckles, and about a half inch down my hand was a deep purple color.

"The shapeshifter stomped on my hand to make me let go of the ledge so we would fall," I spat at him. "It's nothing. It'll heal. I'm fine."

"I don't believe ya. That looks bad, Elisia." Kalvin took a step forward, his eyes never leaving my hand.

"Either way, it'll heal. The perks of being an elf," I dismissed it, hoping he would let the subject pass.

Greyson and Noah approached. I took my hand out of the moonlight and hid it behind my back causally, giving Kalvin a look that told him not to tell. He sighed but complied with my silent request.

"Ready to go?" Noah asked, reaching Kalvin and me.

I nodded and continued walking. We were almost back to the cellar anyway.

The crickets stopped chirping, and footsteps sounded in the dark. Something was running straight at us. I glanced at Kalvin, but he was already moving into position to get behind whatever it was. I took out my blades, pushed Greyson and Noah behind me, and prepared for a fight.

A shadow moved through the forest, looking almost human.

I took a step back and made a quick note of everyone's location. It was two steps from the edge of the brush.

I was ready to charge.

"Elisia!" It was the harsh voice of my father.

I stopped and cringed.

"Dad?" I said, loud enough so Kalvin could hear and wouldn't attack. "What are you doing here?"

Dad looked completely terrifying in the moon-lit forest. "Greyson, Noah, Elisia, come with me. Now!" he demanded, his voice reverberating through the forest.

His nostrils flared as he pointed back the way he came.

We followed him all the way to my backyard where three chairs were positioned on the lawn. I walked over and sat down in the chair furthest away with no need for him to tell me. Noah and Greyson timidly followed and sat down in the other two. My father stood in front of us, arms crossed and lips pursed, a technique that worked on me when I was little. He would stand there, looking exactly like he did then, and I would spill my guts to him.

That time, no one said a word.

He saw it wouldn't work. "Elisia, I am very disappointed in you. Taking a human and someone new to our world into Perfidious is dangerous enough, and to go as far as the base of the mountain..." He took a couple harsh breaths. "And you did it twice. Twice! Noah, your parents thought something happened to you and Greyson when they came home to find you two gone and no word on where you were. Elisia, you're lucky your mother went over there searching for you before they called the police."

He paused, and the guilt set in.

"Elisia, inside," he scolded. "Noah, Greyson, go to the car out front. The story is that you lost track of time studying."

Dad motioned for the boys to follow him. They got up to leave without hesitation. I stood to go inside. Greyson looked at me, opening his mouth to say something but shut it as he looked at my dad. He glanced back at me with sad eyes.

It seemed like he wanted to tell me something but didn't want my father to hear.

I waved to him. "See you at school tomorrow."

Greyson nodded.

Once inside, I stayed in my room and did homework until Dad returned. He was mad at me and probably wouldn't talk to me the rest of the night.

He slammed the door as he walked back in.

"Hey!" I heard Mom yell at him.

"What?" Dad snapped.

"You have no right to treat them like that without an explanation. You don't understand what's going on."

I snuck to my door to sit and listen.

"I know what's going on. Elisia isn't following the rules. She's traveling to places she shouldn't and putting herself in danger. She needs to be disciplined. Maybe we should ground her from Perfidious. See how she acts after a few weeks."

Mom huffed. "Um, no. You may *think* you know what's going on, but you don't. You don't listen to her when she tries to explain herself. You pretend our daughter isn't a half-breed and do everything you can to ignore that fact."

"She shouldn't be a half-breed! She needs to choose which she is."

My breath caught in my lungs.

"No! You want her to be something she isn't. Elisia isn't one or the other. She is both. And she's found friends, humans and half-breeds, that accept her. You can't ground her from Perfidious. I have kept my mouth shut for too long, but I hate what *that place* has done to you."

Silence hung in the air.

"What place, Riley?" Dad's voice was eerily neutral as he spoke to Mom. "And choose your words carefully, because if you're talking about the Council, then—"

"Then what?" Mom was yelling now. "I don't like what they've done to you. Ever since you started there, you've changed. You're not the elf I married or had Elisia with."

I heard footsteps toward my parents' room. Another pair quickly followed. I stood up, ready to make my way to my bed in case they realized I was awake and listening.

"You better not be coming to this room," Mom stated.

"What do you mean?"

"This is my room. I can't handle another night of you waiting around until you think I'm asleep to sneak out and run back to the castle. Either leave now or wait on the couch." Mom slammed her bedroom door.

Dad stood there for a long time, and I was frozen where I was. My parents never really fought, but it wasn't like Dad was ever home for them to have the time to. It kinda made me happy to know that Mom tried to understand me. She didn't know everything going on, but she was right. I was both.

My chest ached. Why did my father think I needed to be one or the other? Was he really letting the Council change his view of half-breeds?

Finally, he moved. I heard him pack up his things and exit through the back door. I tiptoed to my window to watch him stomp into the forest.

I stepped away from the window, ignoring the thoughts scrambling around my head, and looked at the clock. In dim blue letters, it read 12:34. I made my way to the small closet in the living room, quietly grabbed ibuprofen and an ACE bandage, and wrapped it around my hand.

Even though people would be able to tell it was swollen, they'd believe I sprained it without asking too many questions.

Well...as long as no one saw it.

The next morning, I woke to Mom making breakfast. She had peanut butter toast sitting on the table for me, so I plopped in a chair to eat, stopping mid-bite as Mom sat down next to me.

"I'm sorry. I didn't mean to worry you," I said, grabbing a hold of her hand to show her how guilty I felt.

Mom shook her head. "Your father and I talked last night. Don't feel bad for hanging out with your friends. I just want you to tell me something, and I want you to be honest."

I nodded. She took a deep breath. It seemed like she didn't actually want the truth to what she was about to ask.

"Are you going places you shouldn't? Places that are dangerous in Perfidious?"

I wasn't going to lie to her. The fight she had with Dad the night before was probably still on her mind.

"I travelled up to Gross Peak yesterday. It's up on the mountain cliffs. It's further than I should have gone, but I made sure I was with a group. We stayed together and made sure we were safe."

"Why?"

"It was for a friend. I was worried that if I didn't go with him, he would've tried to go himself. He would have ended up dead if he did."

Mom's eyes widened. "I think you know better than to let others influence you, Elisia. You know the rules. You're not allowed to go farther into Perfidious then Coalfell. That's what we agreed upon. It's not safe for someone like you."

That was the problem.

It'd never be safe unless something changed.

I opened and closed my mouth a couple of times to tell her what I wanted to, but nothing came out. Instead, I stood up from the table.

"I need to get to school. I'm not hungry anymore."

I walked past her. My hand ached, and I moved the long sleeve so that it covered the bandage. With one last glance to Mom, I left the house.

I jogged to school and got to Math class before I surfaced from my thoughts. Greyson wasn't at the desk next to mine, and he wasn't in his usual one at the front either.

Where was he?

I wanted to text him, to check in with him, but Mrs. Walker barked at me to take my seat.

I kept looking for Greyson for the rest of the day, but he wasn't at school. If I didn't see him in gym class, I needed to stop by his house to make sure he was okay.

I turned the corner to the locker room just as the creaking janitor door opened next to me.

An arm shot out of the darkness, pulling me inside.

My brain processed everything too slowly for me to react. The person closed the door and put his finger to his lips. I exhaled in relief, seeing who it was.

But I still wanted to slap him.

"Greyson? Why did you—"

He grabbed my left forearm and held my bandaged arm up into the light. I had to tighten my mouth shut to stop from yelping in pain.

"Why didn't you tell me you broke something?"

"I didn't want you to worry about it." I cradled my hand close to my chest.

Why is he so upset?

"Unwrap it. Kalvin taught me something last night."

I hesitated and made a mental note to hit Kalvin the next time I saw him.

"Elisia," he pleaded, "trust me."

I begrudgingly unwrapped the bandage. Even though he hadn't seen it yet, he didn't even flinch at the sight of my broken, battered hand.

He gently placed his palms below and on top of the bruising, watching his hands with intense concentration.

Nothing happened.

What is he trying to do?

I waited impatiently. Gradually, a shiny green light began to glow between us, illuminating most of the small room. A warmth started to spread from my fingers down to my wrist, continuously heating until it felt like fire on my skin. I had to cover my mouth to stop myself from screeching. Each bone popped back into place with a painful snap.

The green light faded, and the purple coloring vanished from my skin.

Greyson wavered on his feet as his eyes struggled to stay open. I held my arms out to steady him before he fell against the wall of toiletries.

"Greyson." I scanned him for any physical injury. "Are you okay?"

He nodded, sweat dripping down his face. "Bones are a lot different from healing a cut. Kalvin came up to my house late last night after your father left. He told me about your hand. He also told me about a fairy who lives in the village with the power to heal. Apparently, Kalvin went to her and asked her to write an explanation of how it works. He cut his arm a few times so I could practice, but healing you took more out of me than I thought it would."

I looked down at my hand, opening and closing it repeatedly, in awe at the lack of pain. I had never been healed before. It differed from my quickened healing, but the result felt like I never broke it.

The bell sounded from the hallway.

"Well, thanks. Now, come on," I said, helping him up and letting him lean on me for support. "Let's get you to the nurse. She'll have something to help you recover."

14

Greyson took small steps to the nurse's office, but he never stopped or hesitated. Sweat seeped through his shirt, sticking to me. I tried to not think about how much it could have cost him.

His eyes glazed over as we hobbled into the clinic. I helped lower him into a chair and made sure he was okay before making my way to Ms. Needham's office.

I'd known Ms. Needham almost all of my life. She was a human doctor who lived in the village to take care of half-breeds but moved to the high school upon my father's request. He wanted to have someone he trusted close to me in case something happened. She responded to house-calls after school and on weekends.

However, since most monsters don't get sick like humans did, Ms. Needham mostly dealt with injuries and overexertion of abilities—which could be deadly but usually only in cases with extreme exhaustion.

I knocked on her office door next to the clinic. The

door was slightly ajar, revealing a filing cabinet and a bookcase on the left that only held a few books. The door creaked as I entered.

"Ms. Needham?" I asked.

An older woman sat at the desk in the middle. Her white coat brought out the white in her usually blonde hair. She looked up from an excessive amount of papers.

"Oh, hello, Elisia. Is something wrong?"

I closed the door behind me to avoid human ears. "Well, I was in Perfidious, as usual, haha." I forced a smile, but her arched eyebrow told me she wasn't buying it. "Um, and I provoked a monster. I ended up breaking my hand. Bad. Like it was shattered in multiple places."

I shivered at the thought.

Her eyes widened as she scanned both of my hands. Not finding an injury, she raised her eyebrows.

I grinned. "You know Greyson, the one in my grade, football player, right?"

"Um, I do. Your father told me he was a half-breed as well. Did something happen to you or him?" Ms. Needham questioned.

I nodded. "Well, he's part fairy. He healed my hand, but it was too much for him to handle. He jumped from healing cuts to shattered bones."

She frowned and grabbed her bag with her herbal treatments and equipment meant for half-breeds and monsters only. I followed her out of her office to where Greyson was sitting. The clinic felt small because of the curtain blocking off the three beds in the back. Ms. Needham grabbed her stool and rolled over to check him out.

"Sorry, Ms. Needham. I know I just saw you a couple

weeks ago for a bump on the head, but I think I hit my head a little too hard this time," Greyson said, trying to make up an excuse.

Ms. Needham laughed. "I didn't know that you could hit your head that hard by healing a broken hand."

Greyson looked from Ms. Needham to me and back again.

"Ms. Needham is human, but she's studied half-breed and monster anatomy. She's helped me with more injuries than I can count," I explained.

Greyson nodded and let her check him out.

She checked all of his vitals—pulse, pupil dilation—and listened to his lungs. Greyson put up with it, but he looked like he just wanted to sleep.

I played with my fingernails. Then, I started to pace.

She had question after question, but she wasn't telling us if he'd be okay. Or if there was really something wrong with him. After all, we did fall from a cliff.

I shook my head. Of course, I was overthinking. I just needed to let Ms. Needham do her job.

Finally, she stood up and turned to me.

I stopped pacing.

"He'll be fine. It wasn't smart, and he needs to learn to start slow." She turned to Greyson as she pulled a small vial out of her bag containing a liquid I knew all too well. "Take this. It's disgusting, but keep it down. Once you drink it all, you will need to sleep. Take the bed all the way in the back. I have to go help someone in Perfidious at 3:30, so I need to leave around 3:00. I'll give Elisia a key so she can come wake you up when she gets out of class."

Greyson nodded and got up to walk back to the bed.

"I'll write you both a pass."

I followed Greyson as Ms. Needham disappeared into her office. He smelled the container and immediately removed it from his face. I giggled under my breath as Greyson brought it to his lips, finishing it with a look of disgust.

"How's it taste?" I asked, already knowing the answer.

Ms. Needham's concoctions never tasted good.

He coughed. "Like she mixed feet, dirty football gear, and—strangely—lime."

"Yeah. I had to take something to speed up my healing process more than a couple times." I laughed more as I took a step back towards the door. "Well, I have to go to class. I'll be back later. Sleep well."

I turned to leave but was pulled back. Greyson's firm grip encased my wrist as he examined my hand.

"Wait, how's your hand?" Greyson asked, looking me straight in the eye.

"Good as new. But you shouldn't worry about that." I said, annoyed that he was still worried about me. He was the one in the nurse's office. "Now, unless you want me to knock you out. Go. To. Sleep." I pushed his chest softly with my newly healed hand so he would get the hint.

Greyson's eyes were so full of warmth as he spoke. "Thanks, Elisia. I'm glad I could help you."

I made sure he laid on the bed and closed his eyes before I left the room. Ms. Needham was waiting outside the door. She handed me the pass with a Cheshire grin. I rolled my eyes.

In the locker room, I quickly changed and made my way into the gym. My usual team sat on the sidelines, Noah anxiously bouncing his knee. His gaze shifted and fell on me, his leg freezing.

I needed to talk to him about Greyson, but first, I handed the gym teacher, Mr. Post, our notes from Ms. Needham.

Noah walked up to me as Mr. Post blew the whistle for the teams to switch. I wanted to talk to Noah, so I made everyone get into a huddle.

"Change of tactics, Anthony and Kyle, take forward and go for the goal. Ryan, play half court. Make sure nothing gets past you. Noah and I will play defense and goalie. We don't have Greyson today, so let's just make sure they don't get a goal," I commanded, and everyone got fired up.

The puck started on our side of the court, but once Anthony got it into offense, he moved around everywhere, trying to get an opening.

"So, where is he?" Noah asked me.

"Did Kalvin come visit you last night?" I countered from the goal.

"Yeah, Greyson said Kalvin wanted to talk to him about something, and then I went back to sleep. Why?"

"Long story short, Kalvin taught him how to heal because he is part fairy. He healed my shattered hand and has to rest in the nurse's office. I have a key to get him out later."

The puck slid past Noah. I smashed the bottom of my stick on top of the puck. It stopped dead. Angling the puck down the court, I passed it to Anthony. He easily got it and aimed for a goal.

"Isn't that dangerous though?" Noah asked.

I forgot he was unaware that Ms. Needham knew. The concept of needing to explain everything twice was frustrating me.

"No. Ms. Needham knows about Perfidious and how to treat us. She is human, but she...Ugh, it's complicated. Just know Greyson is fine and resting."

"So why does he have to rest that much if Kalvin taught him how to do it?" Noah asked.

"Noah. You don't need to worry about Greyson. He's one of us now. We'll take care of him."

I was a little surprised to hear our gym teacher blow the whistle. Our team scored just as the final bell rang. Noah and I stayed behind to put the nets away. After the last person cleared the gym, we were finally able to talk.

It was probably a good thing that I had that time to cool down. I hated being interrogated, which was exactly how Noah was making me feel.

"You really trust them?" Noah started exactly where we left off, but it confused me what he meant.

"Who?" I asked.

"The Elders." He waited for an answer.

I gave him a confused look.

He huffed. "Well, I don't. I only met them once, and they didn't care one bit about finding out who he was. They just put all of their responsibilities on you. In the last few days, Greyson—I guess and me—have gone through a lot. Now Greyson is talking about some heir stuff and wanting to see what the Elders say about it. We should protect him, not put him in front of a crowd with a target on his back. And it won't be humans after him. It will be monsters. Monsters, Elisia! How long do you think we can protect him from that kind of threat?"

I didn't know what to say. Noah was right. I only nodded to show him I understood where he was coming from. It was all I could do. I watched Noah throw his hands up and stomp away.

Honestly, I never thought it would happen in my lifetime. According to Noah, Greyson really believed he was the king's heir. It would be dangerous, but if Greyson *was* the heir, I knew I would follow him.

15

I grabbed my stuff from the locker room. All I wanted to do was go home and take a long, hot shower. I pulled the door open to see Greyson leaning against the wall on the other end of the hallway. He should've still been sleeping in the nurse's office.

I took long strides up to him as he waved to a couple swooning girls down the hall.

"You should still be in bed. How are you feeling?" I asked, looking him over. He wasn't pale, and he seemed to be able to hold himself upright.

He gave me a big smirk. "I feel great. I woke up early. Ms. Needham checked me out and said I was good to go."

I stared at him.

He scratched the back of his head. "She said my healing abilities might be more enhanced than she's seen, which would explain why I woke up early."

"Okay...well," I said slowly, still shocked that he was awake. "I'm glad you're feeling better."

Greyson stood up straighter. "I've been thinking about something, and I need to ask you a question."

"Sure. What's up?"

Greyson opened his mouth to speak, but someone yelled his name.

"Greyson!" Noah stood down the hall, waving. "Let's go. We gotta get to practice."

Greyson nodded. "One sec. I've gotta talk to Elisia about something."

"No," Noah shook his head and quickly made his way to us. "Coach hates it when we're late, right? So, let's go."

Noah started to drag him away.

Greyson looked back at me one more time. He gave me a sad smile. "Catch you later, Elisia."

I walked home and went straight to the bathroom. The shower ran cold as I turned it on. While it warmed up, I found some comfy sweats and a t-shirt. On my way back to the bathroom, I saw a note on my bed from Mom. Probably a list of chores.

The bathroom already had steam pouring out of the door. I stripped down and stepped into the tub, the water burning my skin. I quickly adjusted, letting it wash away my worries.

I didn't even wash my hair until the temperature cooled, the scent of vanilla and strawberries from the shampoo filling the air. I turned the nozzle off and stepped out into the steamed bathroom to dry.

I grabbed the list sitting on my bed. Just my luck...only a couple things on it. I dressed and started on the chores, sweeping all the hardwood floors, taking out the garbage, and making my way to the backyard. My list said I had to rake the leaves, so I searched for the rake on the side of the house.

Rustling leaves came from behind me.

I spun around to face Kalvin running up to me.

He was out of breath. "Elisia..." He stopped running and leaned over slightly. "He went to the Elders. You have to come quick."

My eyes widened as I took a step. "Who went where?"

"Greyson." Kalvin straightened. "The human said he found some sorta proof. He's telling the Elders he's the descendant of the old king." His eyes sparkled, but I saw the concern hiding there.

Greyson should have come to me first.

My feet pounded into the earth almost as fast as my heart was racing. I weaved between the trees, through the gate, and went straight for Coalfell.

What was he telling the Elders? What kind of proof did he have? Butterflies fluttered through my stomach, but I couldn't let myself get too excited. I didn't know if it was true. I needed to see what Greyson had before I believed it.

The outskirts of the town came into view. Trying my best, I maneuvered through the townspeople. A crowd had assembled around the tent, but I shoved past them, making sure Kalvin was still behind me.

Two ogre-looking guards stood outside with Noah. I placed my hand on his shoulder and spun him around.

"What's going on?" I demanded.

Noah shrugged my hand off of his shoulder and pointed harshly at me. "This is your fault. Greyson's been asking my parents a bunch of questions lately about his mom and grandma. Apparently, they had some box left for Greyson from his mom. It explained everything about him being some king's descendent. He wouldn't even talk to me. He just ran right here."

"He what?" I blinked several times and looked behind Noah at the ogres standing at the entrance.

Noah continued talking, but I stopped listening. I sped past the guards, straight into the tent. Greyson was standing in the middle while the Elders whispered amongst themselves. He turned around and gave me a nervous smile. The butterflies in my stomach turned to bees.

For a moment, I forgot I was in the Elders' tent. I went to take a step towards him. He wasn't supposed to be the one that made the rash decisions. What made him decide to go barging in there? What was he thinking? I needed to know what was going on. He should have told me.

Two giant hands closed around my arms and lifted me from the ground.

I snapped out of my internal debate and struggled against them as the ogre went to throw me out.

"Wait!" one of the Elders called.

The guards turned me around, and we faced the Elders.

"She might have just solved our problems. Set her down," Yima said.

The ogre set me down, and I swallowed hard. I made my way next to Greyson, noticing a shoebox in his arms. He stood very still as he watched me, his green eyes beaming but also seeming unsure. Looking into them reminded me that I wasn't there to yell at him. I was there to figure out what was going on and help him.

I turned my attention to the Elders. They looked to one another before addressing the two of us.

Drithro rubbed his temples. "Elisia, we are unsure how much you know, but what we say here is not to be repeated unless we give prior authorization. No one must know. That includes your father." He paused, and I nodded my understanding. "It has been brought to our attention that Greyson is King Lawrence's last living descendent. He has presented us with proof. We need someone to guide and train him if he is to take his rightful place as king someday."

"Wait." Greyson took a step forward. "That's not why I'm here! I wanted to know more about where I came from. Not overthrow—"

Enmah raised her hand. Greyson stopped talking before she spoke. "We're not asking you to do anything hasty, but you want to learn how to use your abilities, don't you?" She didn't give him time to answer. "We are just inquiring that you learn some combat as well. Elisia and Kalvin can teach you."

"Why us? Why not someone with more experience to train the next king?" I looked around for anyone else that could do it.

Yima smiled. "You and Kalvin were trained by Aaron, am I wrong?" I nodded my head, and he continued speaking. "He was the last member of the Guard that we know of, and they were the very best. You and Kalvin *will* train him."

Greyson and I opened our mouths to speak but were cut off.

Drithro spoke clearly and forcefully. "You and Kalvin have been working on ways to improve our safety and security in the village, none of which we have been able to accept as of yet. This is your chance to make a change that we can stand behind."

I sighed. If I refused after he worded it like that, it wouldn't have looked good on my part. "Fine. We'll train him."

Enmah frowned. "No, you will train both of them. The human outside is loyal and protective of his friend. He will make for a great ally in a rebellion."

I took a step forward, but they didn't let me speak.

"It's decided, Elisia! We have nothing else to add. When we have more, we will summon you. Dismissed!" Drithro waved his hand.

The guards shoved us out of the tent.

"Well, that was pointless," Greyson muttered, kicking rocks.

I grabbed his hand. "Let's talk about this somewhere more private."

Kalvin and Noah walked towards us.

"We're going to my cellar."

I didn't want any nosy villagers eavesdropping. We exited the outskirts of the village. Out of hearing distance of prying ears, Greyson whispered to Noah what the Elders said. I tried not to listen. I had enough to think about.

Noah ran in front of all of us and threw his arms into the air. "Stop! This isn't happening. Greyson's not doing this."

"I am, Noah." Greyson spoke definitively. "They just want me to learn how to handle myself. That's all for right now."

Greyson walked past Noah, and we followed him back

to the cellar. He didn't say anything else. His shoulders were tense, and his fists were clenched.

As soon as we got inside, Greyson opened the shoebox to reveal its continents. There was a book called *King's Legacy: Complete History of Perfidious*, a painting of King Lawrence and Miranda, and a letter.

"Noah's mom gave me this. She said my mom gave it to her after I was born. My mom told her that if anything happened to my mom or grandmother, she wanted Mrs. Erikson to adopt me. She put it in her will and everything." Greyson pulled out the letter and handed it to me. "My mom told her to give me the shoebox if I ever started asking a lot of weird questions."

I opened the letter to find multiple pages written in curly handwriting.

Greyson,

My dearest son. I'm sorry I can't be there with you. The fairies believe that when one passes away, they pass their strength to the next in the bloodline. I believe wholeheartedly that I'm with you, some way or another. Your birth wasn't planned, and your father quickly ran away after he found out our secret. That coward.

But there is something you need to know. Something that the Eriksons don't know. You're not entirely human. The birthmark on your shoulder proves that.

I skimmed past the stuff I already explained to Greyson about his Anchor, Perfidious, and what he was. I flipped through to the last page.

. . .

My father, your grandfather, was the last king of Perfidious, which means you have a blood right to the throne. The Council will stop at nothing to see you dead. I have heard rumors that they had turned the peaceful civilization your grandfather worked so hard to build into a grim land tainted with power struggles and death.

On the off chance that you have already learned of this land, your grandmother, Miranda, wanted you to know two things. First, it's your choice to take up the responsibilities of being the heir. You don't have to go for the throne. Second, if you choose to fight, give them hell. Either way, from death we support any decision you make.

Remember, nothing is impossible,
Mom

I looked up from the paper. Greyson's eyes seemed to shine. My mind was swirling to the point I couldn't even form words. It was really happening. Kalvin took the letter from my hands.

Greyson stiffened as he spoke, "So, you two are really gonna train us because Aaron trained you?"

Sadness pinched my heart. I looked to Kalvin who went pale.

"The Elders," Kalvin swallowed, "want us to teach ya 'cause of my dad?"

He seemed to be in his own thoughts, growing quiet. Kalvin suddenly blinked and shook his head.

"Wait." Kalvin looked at me. "Did he just say 'us'? As in him *and* the human?"

I nodded.

Noah butted in before Kalvin could argue. "Wait,

Aaron was your dad? But that would mean he was human, right?"

We all looked at him. Kalvin nodded slightly.

I mentally kicked myself. It wasn't the time to be silent.

"Yes, one of the best fighters," I said. My voice cracked, and I cleared my throat. "The Elders were clear. Training starts tomorrow."

"The Elders are annoying," Greyson mumbled, looking down.

"What?" I asked.

"The Elders expect me to be this king's heir. I don't even know if that's the path I want. I just wanted to learn about my heritage, something about my past." He pushed the shoebox from his lap. "But no. They're too worried about me not being their *problem*. That's why they made me your responsibility. It wasn't because they actually wanted me to learn to fight, but you showed up. You were convenient. Passing off the responsibility to you was too good of an opportunity for them."

I took a step back. My chest ached.

"Hey!" Kalvin got in Greyson's face.

Greyson seemed to want to stand his ground, but his eyes were wide looking up at Kalvin. I held my breath. Kalvin was mad, like actually mad. He usually tried to keep calm and think rationally, but that's not what he looked to be doing.

"That's not the way you talk about someone who has done everything she can to help ya." Kalvin's fists were clenched, but I could tell he was holding himself back. "Now, ya obviously don't realize this, but Elisia and I are the only ones in this village that know what we're doing when it comes to offensive fighting styles. We were the only choice unless ya wanted to get shipped out to some boot camp. So, shut up and be grateful."

The tension released from Greyson's shoulders. He lowered his eyes and nodded at Kalvin, who backed away and stood next to me.

The air filled with awkward silence.

"How about we all head home?" I almost whispered to break the silence. "We can figure out the rest tomorrow. Tonight, we need a good night's sleep."

Everyone nodded and we walked to the gate. From there, Greyson and Noah went to their house, and Kalvin started following me to mine.

"You don't have to walk me home," I said.

Kalvin looked over at me for the first time since we started walking. "I think I need the walk. That guy got on my nerves."

I stayed silent, not sure if I wanted to say what was on my mind. Apparently, my mouth didn't agree.

"You know, you don't have to defend me. I kinda can take care of myself." I made sure my tone was completely joking. I didn't want Kalvin to think I was mad at him.

He threw his head back. "Pff. I know that. I just...I don't know...wanted to make sure he knew that he couldn't talk to ya that way." He turned his head away from me and mumbled. "And I didn't like him calling ya *convenient*."

I smiled and nudged him, but I had to look away before he could tease me about the color changing on my cheeks. It was nice that Kalvin had my back like that.

We entered the clearing of the woods to my backyard. Mom was sitting in her comfy outdoor chair, reading a book. She looked up at us and grinned.

"Kalvin!" Mom put her book down and walked down

the stairs to meet us in the yard. "It's been too long."

Mom hugged Kalvin, but he looked like a trapped animal. His eyes pleaded for me to help him. I just giggled.

"Hi, Mrs. Meyer. I was just walking Elisia home," Kalvin said.

"Nonsense! Do you want some dinner? I made plenty. I thought my daughter would be home." Mom turned her attention to me.

I shrugged. "I thought I would be too, but the Elders needed me."

"Mhm." Mom didn't believe me but turned back to Kalvin, dragging him inside the house.

Kalvin didn't come over much and that was why. My mom wasn't like Tamara—strong, bold, or outspoken. My mom was overly motherly. She always tried to feed Kalvin and ask about his personal life. He didn't hate it, but it did make him uncomfortable. I wished Kalvin was able to come over more, but he didn't like being outside of Perfidious. Coming to my house was the furthest he'd go.

Kalvin gobbled down a plate of food before telling my mom he had to go. He used the excuse of having to work at the blacksmith shop early. I watched him walk into the woods, waving at me even though he didn't see me at the window.

16

In the morning, I texted Greyson to bring the letter to school.

I read it start to finish. Then, I read it again. It *was* happening! I couldn't believe it. Greyson really was the heir. And *I* was going to train him.

School felt surreal. Going to class after class felt too normal after all the events of the night before. I never imagined that I would be part of the revolution that changed Perfidious. It wasn't something that had crossed my mind, but after being made part of it, I knew I was exactly where I was meant to be.

I wrote down all the things that would need to be done. We'd need to train Greyson and Noah to fight. Kalvin knew most of his dad's techniques and was a great fighter. I was probably getting in over my head, but I needed to get my excitement out and on paper so I would focus on the task at hand—training. Just training. Not overthrowing the Council. That wasn't even on the table yet. But just in case,

Greyson and Noah needed to be prepared for anything and everything.

The bell rang, pulling me from my train of thought.

I shoved the paper into my notebook and ran to gym class. By the time I changed, everyone was already ready, and the teacher was looking at a clipboard. I approached him.

"Mr. Post, can I ask a favor? I noticed that we're scheduled to play Team 6 today, but they haven't won a game and my team hasn't lost one."

"What's your point, Elisia?" He lowered his clipboard.

"I was wondering if, only for this game, I could switch teams so that they would have a chance of winning a game?"

He stroked his chin but remained silent.

I batted my eyes. "Please? Just one game?"

"Sure." He blew the whistle around his neck, and his voice echoed in the open gym. "Team 6 vs. Team 3."

Confusion spread across the room as I joined Team 6 instead of Team 3.

Greyson and I met in the middle to shake hands. He opened his mouth to talk, but I whispered before he could speak.

"It's only for one game. Training starts now. Get it past me just once between you and Noah. If you don't, I'll make you pay for it in sprints after school." I smirked.

Greyson smiled, accepting the challenge. His hand tightened around mine. "Deal, but what if we get it past you? What will we get?"

I started walking away. "You're already in line to become king. What else could you want?"

I turned around to talk to my temporary team.

Instead of coming in for a huddle, my new team stood around talking or just zoning out. I tried to get them to head to the other end of the makeshift court, but they barely moved over half court. I took my stance as the only defender.

The puck dropped. Greyson reacted faster than the human across from him. He ran toward me.

I took my hockey stick and hit it out from under him. Greyson's head snapped from side to side as he looked for the puck. I snickered.

This will be fun.

For me, at least.

I increased my speed just past what was normal to humans. I tried it on Noah first. He blinked a few times, unable to really follow my movements.

Put on *To Teach* list: teach Noah to track monsters.

Kalvin was pretty good at predicting others' movements. I'd have him work on that with Noah.

I tried the move on Greyson, who was able to mimic me. His speed was just as fast as mine, but I still outsmarted him to get the puck back on the other side of the court.

Our teacher blew the whistle.

I felt disappointed. I was actually having a lot of fun. Watching the next game, they joked about how they could have gotten it past me if they had more time, but I knew there was no way.

Taking turns trying to get it around me was futile. Yet, if they actually teamed up and outnumbered me, they might have won. Once they learned how to fight, they'd make a great team. Maybe the Elders had the right idea to train them both.

After school, Greyson and Noah told their coach they had important appointments, and they wouldn't be at practices for the next few days. The coach didn't seem happy, but he let them go.

We walked straight to the root cellar to meet Kalvin.

However, Kalvin wasn't waiting outside for us. I motioned for the boys to stop talking as I listened to my surroundings. Birds chirped, but no critters rustled the underbrush. My instincts kicked in.

I ran to the small door in the ground, opened the door, and reached down to grab one of my blades. I pulled the small handle, letting the blade swing into its natural position along the length of my forearm. I turned around in time to catch Kalvin's blade a few inches from my face. I reached behind me to grab my second blade and pushed Kalvin back with my legs.

There was barely time to stand. The sword's point came down near my chest. I turned my left blade, facing it away from my body. I leveraged to push Kalvin's blade away from me to my left and down. Kalvin's body weight followed the sword as it struck into the ground.

I felt a sting in my arm as I backed away. It looked like the blade nicked me a little, but it would heal in the next couple of hours. I still needed to get used to my weapons.

I watched as Kalvin's narrow pupils returned to the human round, signaling the end of the fight. Normally, we would continue until someone tapped out, but as he turned his attention to Greyson and Noah, I realized he was just using the exercise as an example.

Kalvin spoke with the same conviction his father had when he told us, "From here to the edge of the forest, excluding the village, will be the area in which we will train. Your training begins the moment you enter this area, which includes sneak attacks if you couldn't tell. During training, you will stay within the limits. Is this clear?"

Noah nodded. "As long as you teach me to fight like that, I'll listen to almost anything." Noah turned to Greyson, some concern showing in his facial expression. "You ready for this, Greyson?"

Greyson's eyes were hazed over as he met my eyes, his mind obviously somewhere else. He smiled at Noah. "Yeah."

I told Kalvin I wanted him to work with Noah's instincts, sharpening them to pick up on monster movements. Kalvin agreed and told me to work with Greyson on getting his stamina up for using his abilities.

Greyson walked up to me as Kalvin pulled Noah aside.

"How about we start with you shifting your shoulder blades into wings?" I placed my hands on my hips and hoped I looked like I knew what I was talking about.

He reached for my hand. "I think I'll start with healing."

I realized there was a trail of blood dripping down my arm. The cut was bleeding more than I thought.

Greyson put his hand over the cut. I watched as he concentrated, a green glow coming from underneath his hand. My skin warmed. Greyson's eyes were intent on not looking anywhere other than my arm.

"I'm sorry about yesterday. I didn't mean it like that...I was just upset," Greyson said. His eyes flashed to mine and back to my arm.

He removed his hand. The cut was gone, only a bloody handprint remaining.

"It's okay. I understand. And thanks." I motioned to my

arm as I reached down into the cellar for a towel to wipe the blood off.

"No problem."

But I knew it was. I could tell he was tired just from using a small amount of his healing ability.

We worked on defensive hand-to-hand combat along with the sprints I'd promised them. I didn't want him overexerting himself from using his powers again.

A couple hours passed, and darkness began to consume the forest. We had to call it quits for the night. Greyson and Noah could barely see, and their arms hung limp at their sides. Kalvin wanted to walk us home again, but I told him he didn't have to. He needed rest.

After Kalvin finally left, I dropped Greyson and Noah off and headed for home. I walked in through the front door and found Mom washing dishes in the kitchen.

Her head remained down.

"Did I miss dinner?" I asked apologetically.

"Yes. You did. I didn't know you would be out so late. Again." She rubbed her eyebrows as she spoke, but she didn't move her gaze from the dishes.

"Sorry, I was hanging out with Kalvin and some new friends. It was actually a lot of fun."

Mom shifted. She cocked her head towards me. "Your father keeps telling me that you're not being safe. That we need to ground you from Perfidious to see if you learn a lesson. You're never home, and I don't know where you've been." She finally turned and I could see the concern in her eyes. "On the other hand, I don't want to see you separated from your friends. What do you think I should decide?

"Mom..." I didn't know how to respond. Mom didn't

understand what was going on in my life. I took a deep breath. "I'm sorry I haven't been home. I was in Coalfell. I promise, Mom. I haven't been anywhere dangerous. I've just been hanging out with Kalvin, Greyson, and Noah."

"That's all?"

"Yes, Mom. I promise."

Her shoulders relaxed, and she seemed to be satisfied with my response. Her eyes softened. "I'm choosing to trust you, but I want to know where you are from now on. And if I find out that you've lied to me about the smallest thing, you will lose my trust."

I nodded.

She pointed to the fridge. "Anyway, I set aside a plate for you. It might still be warm."

I grabbed the plate and sat with my mom while I ate. We talked a bit, and I realized just how much I'd been gone. I felt bad, but I promised her I would try to make it back for dinner from then on. After I ate, I changed and crawled into bed. It had been a long day and the next wouldn't be any easier.

17

The next school day couldn't have passed by fast enough. I saw Noah and Greyson a few times and could tell Greyson looked more tired than usual. However, I was surprised that neither of them seemed sore.

After school got out, Greyson, Noah, and I dropped our stuff off at our houses and entered the forest to meet Kalvin.

"So, how sore are you guys today?" I asked.

Noah snickered, and Greyson tried to hold back a grin.

"What did you do?" I asked, arching my eyebrow.

"Nothing really," Greyson answered me, no longer hiding his smile. "Noah could barely move this morning, and I only felt a little sore. Figured my body healed itself faster. So, I attempted to heal Noah's muscles and my own. It was different from a cut, and it used less energy, but it still worked on him. I found out I can't heal myself."

I realized that could have been the reason he looked tired, but I let it pass. "As long as you're careful. You know how healing can drain you."

He nodded sincerely, and that was good enough for me.

"Oh, I keep forgetting. Remember when I made you use the wings to save us from falling?"

Greyson nodded.

"Well, I wasn't entirely sure that it would work. But I'm glad it did."

He didn't even pretend to be surprised. "Honestly, I was surprised you even suggested it. What made you think I could do it?"

"Your legs." I realized it was a bad explanation the moment I said it. "When we were running away from the shapeshifter, I was running at full speed with my elf abilities. You stayed with me, which made me think you've been subconsciously changing the muscles in your legs to resemble an elf's for a while. I mean we've been in the same class forever. You could have easily seen how fast I could run and wanted to run faster than you were. The desire could have caused you to alter the muscles in your legs so you could do that."

Greyson seemed interested.

"Now that I know the truth about you being an elf, I can see how much you hold back in gym," Greyson nudged me playfully. "So, if I've been able to run as fast as you all this time, then why haven't I? I mean, I do a lot of running at football practice, and Coach likes to push us to our limits."

I thought about this for a second, but I didn't have a definite answer. "I'm not sure. If I had to take a guess, I'd say that it was more a mental block. You didn't know about anything outside of being a human. You believed humans could only run so fast, so you didn't exceed that limit. Maybe?"

Noah was jerked away from us.

I turned to see Kalvin putting him into a choke hold. Noah positioned his chin down and pulled on Kalvin's arm. Kalvin simply smiled as Noah leaned down, threatening to pull Kalvin over his shoulder. He shifted position, letting go of the choke hold, and used Noah's momentum against him, putting his arm under Noah's waist and flipping him over. Noah landed in the grass.

Thud.

I cringed at Noah's defeat. He did really well and learned a lot in a day, but he had a long way to go before he could win against Kalvin. I didn't think I'd even win against Kalvin if we were fighting for real.

Kalvin clapped and offered his hand to Noah. "Good try. Ya did it exactly right. Next time, ya'll need to adjust to the change of position." He looked at me. "So, what're we doin' today, Elisia?"

When did I become the head trainer? I rolled my eyes. I guess it didn't matter. I had a plan anyway.

"Kalvin, I want you to help Greyson with his shifting. We already know he can change his shoulder blades to wings and the muscles in his legs to resemble an elf's. Can you teach him to change his eyes to enhance his eyesight like yours? Or even his skin to dragon skin?"

Kalvin nodded. "Sure, that sounds like a good idea. I'll take him to the blacksmith shop. There was a lot of traffic coming in and out while I was working earlier. Who knows how many abilities he can pick up by shaking hands."

Greyson frowned. "I don't think I can just touch

someone to gain their abilities. I have to be able to understand how it feels like and how it works."

"That we can figure out later. It'd still be good to make
contact with others so ya have the possibility to pick up
some skills." Kalvin met my eyes. "What about Noah?"

I bit my lip. I hadn't actually thought about Noah's
training. Kalvin picked up on this.

"How about ya take him to Antheia's bookstore? She'll
have some books that can teach him about the different
abilities he'll need to work around."

"Isn't Antheia's far?" I asked, not remembering where it
was exactly.

"It's only two miles, if that. North past the Mourning
Willow, remember?" Kalvin directed.

I nodded. "Oh yeah. Come on, Noah. It shouldn't take
us more than 40 minutes to get there."

Noah followed me to Antheia's. Awkward silence hung
between us. I had no idea what to say to him. Every time
I'd talked to him in the last couple of days, we seemed to
fight, and I really didn't want to fight with him. We were
both friends with Greyson, but it seemed like we would
never be friends with each other at the rate we were going.

He stayed with me as he watched his surroundings,
never looking my way. His eyes widened at something
ahead of us.

The Mourning Willow stood tall against the evening
sun and seemed to shimmer from the light hitting all the
trinkets inside.

"What's this?" Noah asked, ducking under the willow
branches.

"It's for all the half-breeds who were killed by
monsters. Their families will never know justice, so this is

here for them to know that they aren't alone." I lowered my head and stepped over a couple roots.

"Aren't there laws to prevent any of this? What about the Coalfell Elders? They're half-breeds. Shouldn't they have laws against that?" His voice fell flat as he spoke.

"The Coalfell Elders only help manage Coalfell. The rulers of Perfidious are called the Council. They could care less about half-breeds. To them, we're just impure parasites. All they care about are the purebloods. If one of them was killed, there'd be a full investigation. But us? Nope. Just one less parasite roaming the land."

My nails dug into the palms of my hands. I hated the Council. If the King's bloodline was still in power, Perfidious wouldn't be that way.

"Is it really that dangerous for all of you here? Why don't you just leave?"

"Not everyone can. Greyson and I are lucky. We can pass for humans. But for others like Kalvin...they have a hard time not drawing attention to themselves," I said as we left the willow.

"Is that why you learned to fight?"

I nodded. "For the most part. I started training because my father wanted me to learn the basics. He said it would be good for me to know how to defend myself, but he got too busy with his job. That's why I started training with Aaron. After I met Kalvin and his father, I convinced him to train me." I paused, shaking my head. I was getting away from his question. "We train because it's fun. Kalvin and I both love it, but it's mostly for survival."

"So, does Kalvin go to school, or is there even school in Perfidious?"

Normally, all of Noah's questions bothered me, but for

the first time, he seemed genuinely curious and not judgmental.

"No, Kalvin has a job with a blacksmith in Coalfell. Most half-breeds are homeschooled. There's someone in town that will hold classes on different topics, but other than that, books and experience are the best option."

"I'm guessing that's why we're headed to a bookstore, right?"

I nodded.

Noah didn't say anything for a long time. His head hung low and his lips thinned as though a debate were batting around his head.

It wasn't a long walk from the Mourning Willow to Antheia's bookstore. Antheia, a griffin, stood behind the counter. Light brown feathers covered her body, and as soon as she saw me, she waved with her paw. I waved back and turned to Noah, who was trying not to stare.

"Is that a human with you?" Antheia asked, her snout sniffing the air.

"Yes, but don't worry, we'll be quick." I nudged Noah to walk to the back of the store where the larger shelves were.

"Okay," she called behind us. "As long as he doesn't cause problems."

I rolled my eyes as I whispered to him. "She's just worried your scent will attract monsters."

"Is she a griffin? I thought they were supposed to be bigger," Noah asked. His eyes still hadn't left Antheia.

"She's only 30 something. Griffin's don't normally become full grown until 50 or 60 years," I said, beginning to scan the shelves.

Noah's brow furrowed.

"Time moves differently for monsters and half-breeds.

Purebloods can live well over a few hundred years. What humans consider to be a long life are basically the baby years for most monsters," I explained.

While I looked for specific books that had helped me with my own training, Noah pulled out a monster book. I saw him shift with uncertainty with every page he flipped, finally slamming the book shut and putting it back on the shelf. He noticed me looking.

"Um, Elisia, are all the monsters in folklore and mythology real?"

"It's hard to tell. There used to be thousands before the monsters got into a war with the humans. Many monsters became extinct before the kings signed the treaty." I returned my attention to the bookshelf, looking down at the covers.

A book with a silver lining around its copper cover caught my eye. I pulled it from the shelf and opened to a random page. It contained knowledge of pureblood abilities and abilities that would be passed down to half-breeds. The author interviewed someone from each species, but I'm sure some monsters wouldn't have told him everything. Still, it would be very helpful in training.

I handed the book to Noah. His eyes danced around the room but stopped at nothing in particular.

I sighed and stopped what I was doing. "What's on your mind?"

Noah looked up with wide eyes. "I think the Elders in Coalfell are lazy." He spoke quickly. "I mean, they listened to Greyson for around fifteen minutes before you showed up. Then they hand over the responsibility to you, so they don't have to deal with it. On top of that, they tell you to train me, a human, because they know I won't leave him.

But how would I be able to deal with these things, like dragons and ogres? Half-breeds can barely survive in this world, right?"

Noah's face was pale as he held the book tightly. He seemed intrigued at first about dragons and elves being real. Yet, it wasn't all unicorns and rainbows. The world we were in was really dangerous, and he finally appeared to be understanding. If he was going to be scared, he could end up hurting Greyson. I needed to say something to give him confidence.

"So? How does being human cripple you? Hundreds of years ago, humans were slaying monsters like the dragons. They nearly brought us to extinction." His wide eyes held mine as I spoke. "Plus, Aaron excelled as a member of the Guard while it existed."

Noah tilted his head to the side and pursed his lips. "What was the Guard? No one has really explained."

"The Guard was what King Lawrence called his army. They were supposedly disbanded when he was killed since they were only loyal to the king's bloodline, but they secretly still had a couple camps that trained new members. Just in case the heir returned and needed an army, you know. The Council eventually found out and wiped out the camps."

"So then how does Aaron fit into this?" Noah looked at his hands as if he was seeing them for the first time.

"Aaron was at one of the camps but left after his training was completed because of Tamara being pregnant with Kalvin."

"Why would they train a human?"

I arched my eyebrow at him.

"I mean, it's not like humans are strong here," he

continued. "Humans seem to be pretty low on the food chain. So why would they train them?"

"Well." I tried to remember the stories Aaron told me. "Most humans wouldn't have been let in. The Guard really only consisted of half-breeds and purebloods, but Aaron showed persistence, determination, and loyalty. Those were some of the traits that every member of the Guard valued. So, they gave him a spot in the camp and started training him."

It wasn't easy talking about Kalvin's dad. I missed him a lot. Aaron told lots of stories before he was killed. Never of battles, but of family and overcoming hardship.

Noah nodded even though I didn't ask a question. He raised his head, and I realized his demeanor had changed. His shoulders straightened, and his eyes weren't shaking. Instead, he was standing tall and strong. It made me glad to know what I told him had helped.

"So, are you looking for specific books, or are you just looking?" Noah asked, letting the subject drop completely.

"A little of both. I'm looking for two certain books. I found one, but I also need one that lists the extinct monsters and their abilities. The one I already handed you only has the monsters currently living." I pulled out every book only to place it back in the same spot.

"I'll go ask," Noah offered. He didn't even wait for me to respond before he walked away.

Antheia had to track down the book in the back. Since few people read it, she'd taken it off the shelves. Once she found it, we paid and left.

I left Noah alone on the walk back. He had a lot to think about. I decided it'd be better to leave him to work it out. I had hope he'd eventually find his footing.

We reached my root cellar by the oak just before seven. I went to put the books in the room, but Noah wouldn't hand them over.

"I'll take them home." He held the books tight to his body. "I wanna look them over tonight."

I rolled my eyes and put my weapons inside the door. My phone glowed to life as I powered it up. One message from Greyson popped up on my screen.

Went back home. Kalvin said I was done for the day and made sure I knew the path before letting me go. Catch you 2morrow.

I showed Noah the text before I led him back to his house. I made it home just in time for dinner. By the time I was ready for bed, I was so exhausted I passed out as soon as my head hit the pillow.

In 1653, the Shapeshifter King found a shapeshifter boy named Lawrence trying to steal from the castle kitchen. The king discovered the boy had been an orphan and was only eighteen years old. He took him in as his adopted son.

The Shapeshifter King fell ill as of late December 1762. He declared Lawrence his heir, hoping the young shifter would keep it the safe haven he tried to create. The king died on November 16th, 1764 at age 562.

There were many obstacles that King Lawrence had to face after his coronation, but he faced them alone. He didn't know what kind of repercussions could occur from trusting the wrong person. Perfidious had become an area of peace for the monsters. King Lawrence's job was to continue that legacy.

However, things started to change when he met the love of his life, a fairy that worked in the castle library, Miranda. They began their courtship in 1845, the same year riots broke out in multiple places of Perfidious over the existence of half-breeds. King Lawrence's loyal army, called the Guard, kept them under control, and they stopped soon after they started. But King Lawrence knew peace wouldn't last long after his decision to continue courting Miranda.

An excerpt from The King's Legacy:
A Complete History of Perfidious

18

My father charged, his spear aimed at my chest. I swung my blade around to knock the spear from its path and planted my feet into the ground. I didn't want to attack, but I wouldn't stop defending myself. He charged at me again in the same position, and I blocked it. He used the momentum of his spear to spin it around, knocking my blade from my hand. He kicked me in the stomach. I landed on the ground, hard. Cold metal pressed against my chin. I looked up to see my father's spear pointed at my throat.

I shot up in bed. Sweaty clothes stuck to my skin. I choked on air as it entered my lungs. Even though it became easier to breathe, I could still feel the spear on my throat.

I ran to the bathroom. My reflection stared at me in the mirror, unharmed. I wasn't sure what I expected to see.

It was a dream. Just a dream.

I hopped into the cold shower to shock myself back into reality. Closing my eyes, I tried to empty my mind, but I couldn't shake the feeling of cold metal on my skin. Why would I dream about that? Maybe it had something to do with all the time I'd been spending thinking about the king's heir. My father wouldn't approve. He'd probably be furious.

The day passed by in a blink. School, training, bed. It was becoming a pattern. By Saturday, I was expecting a break from the training, but I was wrong.

Kalvin wanted to spend the day sparring, with me only using my new blades. According to him, I needed to get used to their twirling motion. I kept bending my wrist wrong and nicking my arms with the tips. Kalvin tried to make a pair for practice while he was working at the blacksmith shop, but he hadn't been successful.

We finished the night how we usually did, with Greyson healing Noah's bruises and my shallow cuts. It seemed like healing was going easier for him. He didn't need to concentrate as hard for the green light to start, and he wasn't as tired afterwards, but it still drained him. I didn't like seeing him use so much energy. But that's why we only let him heal at the end of practice.

Kalvin insisted on walking me home. We were too tired to talk, but we didn't need to. Just having him there always made me feel better. He winked at me as we were nearing my house.

I walked into the clearing that was my backyard, but Kalvin stopped.

"You wanna come in? There are plenty of leftovers, and I'm sure everything in my fridge is better than what's in yours," I teased.

Kalvin flashed a smile but hunched his shoulders as he slid his hands into his pockets. "I would, but I, uh, shouldn't. Just tell your parents I said hi. I should go."

He turned around before I could protest. I waved to his back. Kalvin knew me well enough to wave as he disappeared into the woods. I walked inside and noticed the difference in the atmosphere. It turned thick with tension. I turned the corner to find my father sitting at the table, tapping his foot.

That explained Kalvin's weird behavior. He never liked my father.

My father didn't look up. "This entire week I looked forward to spending the day with my family. Only to find out you're suddenly never home and your mother doesn't know where you've been." My father frowned as he looked up. "Care to explain?"

"Not particularly." I told him, walking further into the kitchen. "I already discussed it with Mom. We worked things out. She said it was fine as long as I told her where I was and who I was with."

My father got up and took a step closer to me. He made eye contact with me to use his ability. Did he really not trust me that much?

"Where have you been?" His voice was stern.

What was he getting angry about?

"My root cellar. Kalvin, Greyson, Noah and I have been hanging out there a lot lately."

"Why?" He barked.

"We've been training." I gave the short answers, but the moment his questions got more specific, the truth would come out. I just didn't know how he'd take it.

"What for?" He asked, growing more impatient.

"Just training. The Elders demanded that I train them, so I'm doing what they told me to do. Why all the questions?"

He tilted his head and his voice lost some of the anger "Why train them? Noah's just a human, and Greyson should learn what he is, not combat. Why would the Elders demand that you train them?"

I closed the cupboard harder than I should. "We know what Greyson is. He has been learning how to use his abilities. They are also in Perfidious a lot. Is it wrong for them to learn to defend themselves? It's not like anyone else'll protect us."

My hands clenched at my side. I knew the last comment was unnecessary, but I didn't care.

"Yes, but you've never trained this much in the past. Why train this hard now?" His eyes narrowed as he crossed his arms and took a step forward.

He was interrogating me again, and I didn't like it.

I spoke through clenched teeth. "Why would you care?"

I opened the fridge, and he closed it immediately. "You will answer my questions fully and truthfully, Elisia! I'm sick of your vague, short answers. If you don't tell me what I want to know I'll—"

"You'll what!" I challenged. "Ground me? You're never home. You don't even stay a full night anymore. You wait until Mom is asleep and then sneak out."

"Enough, Elisia! Tell me what I want to hear. Tell me the truth." He raised his voice.

"Which do you want then? What you want to hear or the truth? You're not gonna get both," I said, standing tall.

I wasn't sure if it was from my dream the night before,

but I was tired of defending myself. He always asked me ridiculous questions. He never trusted me.

"Elisia!"

"Fine! The Coalfell Elders want Kalvin and I to train them because we found out that Greyson is part fairy and part shapeshifter." I saw realization dawn in my father's eyes. He knew what that meant. "He is King Lawrence's grandson, the last living heir. They want him to be ready when the day comes for him to take his rightful place on the throne. The Council does nothing for half-breeds! Things need to change."

His entire body tensed, and his nostrils flared. "You will not speak of our rulers with such ill manners! They are understanding. If they weren't, I'd never have been able to work at the castle, let alone hold a position in the court." My father had always a great amount of respect for the Council, not that I understood why.

I pulled at my hair. I needed him to understand my side for once. Maybe if I explained how I felt, he'd see what I was trying to accomplish.

"But they don't keep anyone safe! The Council doesn't understand how the half-breeds feel or even care about what we're going through. Half-breeds, like me, are murdered, and no one does anything to stop it. I'm trying to help change things for the better. Then Perfidious wouldn't be so divided."

He took a couple steps back as though I physically struck him.

"How could you betray me like this? I have been talking you up to the Council so that someday they might let you work for them as I do. But you really need to think about your actions if this is the path you want to go down—"

"How have I betrayed you? The Council would never let me work for them. I'm not just an elf. I'm a *half-breed*. I want Perfidious to be safer for people like me. Wouldn't you want it safer for your daughter?"

I had no clue what was going through his head. He was making it about him and the Council, making it seem as though I was in the wrong. Again! I wasn't good enough for him. Mom was right. Working at the Council had changed him.

It wasn't a quick change, but over the years he had become less understanding of what I was and what I was going though. I didn't think he'd ever see my side, not after working in a place that saw half-breeds as impure parasites.

My father straightened and slammed his fist on the kitchen counter, causing me to jump. "That's enough, Elisia! Maybe Perfidious isn't a place for you. You are part human and look human. If you think it's so dangerous, then maybe you need to stay out of Perfidious." His words were harsh, as though what he said was law. "You want life to be safer? I'll make it simple for you. You're grounded. You're not allowed to step foot in Perfidious. I will hire a scout to monitor you at all times to make sure you obey these new rules."

"What? No! Perfidious is my home! You can't take that away from me!" I yelled.

He was the one betraying me, not the other way around.

My father crossed his arms. "Not if you're training

someone to overthrow the Council. You do not understand what that would do. It would change everything!"

"That's the idea." I started to walk away, but he grabbed my arm.

"Where are you going?" He demanded.

I ripped my arm out of his grip. "Away from you."

"Elisia Meyer, half-breeds don't belong in this world. They never have. You should understand this by now."

I froze. He had crossed a line.

Tears stung my eyes as I stomped into my room, slamming the door shut behind me. A sickening crack vibrated through the door. I had probably broken it. I would apologize to Mom later.

I didn't know the person standing in the kitchen. It clearly wasn't my father. That man was different, acting like all the other pureblooded monsters. My father taught me that I was a strong elf, whether I was a half-breed or not. Working at the castle had ruined him. Until I recognized him as the father I once knew, he didn't deserve to be called my father. From then on, he was just Erlan to me.

My vision became blurry as tears threatened to pour from my eyes. I wiped at them angrily. I couldn't cry. Not yet. First, I needed to get out of the house.

I grabbed a bag and started shoving random clothes into its empty pockets, packing everything I thought I would need so I wouldn't have to come back. Mom wouldn't know what happened to me, but I wrote her a note telling her that I was going to stay in Coalfell for a couple of days.

I left the note on my bed and quickly learned that my door really was stuck. My window would probably be better anyway. I didn't know if *Erlan* was still there.

I exited the house, still numb from the conversation. I walked all the way to Kalvin's house and knocked on the door until Kalvin opened it. I looked at his messy black hair, his cutoff T-shirt, and his long green sweatpants. His fiery orange eyes observed me with concern. I saw his lips moving, but I couldn't hear what he was saying.

Tears started steaming down my face uncontrollably.

Kalvin pulled me inside and let me cry into his chest, holding me in his arms. My body felt weak, and I almost collapsed to the ground. Kalvin picked me up and moved us to the couch nearest the door. He didn't have to say anything to comfort me, and he knew it.

After what felt like hours of crying, I finally started to calm down and explained to Kalvin what had happened. He helped me remove my backpack and my shoes. After placing them in a closet, he came back to me. I think he asked me if I wanted to go to sleep, but my mind wasn't comprehending much.

I stopped crying, but it felt like my brain wouldn't work anymore. Without me giving him an answer, he half carried, half helped me walk into his bedroom. I laid down on his soft bed just as the rest of my tears seeped from my eyes. I felt the bed shift as Kalvin laid down next to me. He held me as I cried myself to sleep.

19

I woke up tangled within the covers of Kalvin's bed. Alone, I got up and looked around. The bathroom mirror showed my reflection, but I wished it hadn't. Red eyes and tear-stained cheeks looked back at me. I splashed water on my face and stood there, eyes closed. The thoughts swirling around my head weren't helping my mood, so I pushed them down and looked back in the mirror. My eyes looked lifeless, but it was better than sad.

I walked into the kitchen area. Kalvin's small house was the size of an apartment. The kitchen had some counters and a small round table. A small, covered plate sat on the table, a note in Kalvin's messy handwriting on top.

Elisia,

There isn't much food in the house. Sorry, but I know you like cinnamon rolls. I left to meet Greyson and Noah to train them more and give you some time. If someone knocks on the door, don't answer it, just in case it's your dad.

Kalvin

I smiled, feeling something for the first time since I got out of bed. A medium-sized cinnamon roll sat beneath the plate. I took a bite, not thinking about where he got it. As soon as the cinnamony goodness touched my tongue, I knew it was from the bakery nearby. They had the best pastries. I mentally reminded myself that I needed to thank him the next time I saw him.

I quickly changed and left his house, still eating the treat. It felt like I was getting judgmental stares as I walked through Coalfell, so I increased my pace. Once I was surrounded by trees, it was easier to breathe. I walked the extra couple of minutes to my bunker.

No one noticed me at first. Greyson and Noah were practicing their daily routines with the swords. Kalvin sat watching their movements, pointing mistakes out every now and then.

I slowed down my pace. What was I going to say to them? I really didn't want to tell them anything. I didn't even want to believe the fight happened.

As if he heard my thoughts, Kalvin glanced at me and stood up. Greyson and Noah caught on and looked at me as well. All of their eyes on me made my skin crawl.

"Spar for a bit," Kalvin said, finally removing his eyes from me. "We'll work on more stuff later. Also, Greyson, try to keep the dragon skin on, okay? You can't heal yourself."

Greyson nodded. He and Noah faced each other. I watched the way they moved and compared it to the way they had fought only a week before. They were already drastically improving.

"Elisia, we're gonna spar." Kalvin lifted his shirt to reveal the sheathed medieval dagger.

"Fine, I'll grab my blades." I jumped down into the trap door of the cellar, but I heard Kalvin above me.

"You know they have a name, right?" He smiled, looking down at me through the door.

Kalvin looked cute as he looked down at me. His black hair hung down, and he was wearing a cut off t-shirt that showed off his muscles.

"No, what are they called?" I asked, but any curiosity I had didn't show in my voice.

"They're called Tonfa blades, or just Tonfas," he clarified as he helped me out of the room.

"Hm." I tried to show interest, but the fight with my father still invaded my thoughts.

Kalvin frowned as he widened his stance. He unsheathed his dagger and held it like an ice pick. Usually, I was eager to start the fight, but not that day. Kalvin lunged. I turned the blade pointing out and moved his blade to the left of me. His attack missed my body by a mile.

His next strike was more precise. He came from above. I reacted by blocking his path with my tonfa on my arm. Kalvin dropped the blade from his left to his right as he stabbed upwards instead. It surprised me, but I moved my arm in a semicircle, knocking his blade to the side.

Kalvin stopped and placed his hand on his hip. "Come on, Elisia," he begged, "sparring will make ya feel better."

I didn't respond with words. I lifted my tonfas and slid my foot out, preparing for an attack. Kalvin grinned and motioned for me to attack first. I fought more aggressively than I had during any spar, which meant I was sloppy. Kalvin didn't point it out, but I knew.

After a lot of aimless swinging, I noticed I hadn't touched him. My competitive spirit compelled me to get the upper hand and try to win. I stopped for a second and started to think about technique. The next time I went in, I focused my strength on getting Kalvin's blade away from him.

I angled both of my Tonfas facing away from my body. As I had anticipated, Kalvin came down with his blade in a stabbing motion. I blocked it with my right and brought my left Tonfa over top of his, capturing the blade between the two. I pushed down with my left and pulled up with my right. Kalvin easily released the sword as it flung over my head.

I started celebrating my victory too soon.

Kalvin kicked me down before I could react. He pinned my left arm, digging the blade of my tonfa into the grass. He placed his other hand between my tonfa and arm, using his position to point the blade's tip near my chest.

I relaxed underneath him. He accepted it as a sign of defeat and helped me up.

Crimson dripped from his other hand.

"Kalvin, your hand," I exclaimed.

He looked down at his hand with a shrug. "Yup, I forgot my mom made your weapons sharp enough to cut me. It'll heal within the next day."

"I can heal that!" Greyson yelled over to us. He put his sword down and jogged over.

Kalvin put his hand behind his back and forced a smile at Greyson. "Nah, I'm good."

Greyson laughed. "Is the big dragon scared of healing?"

Kalvin frowned, only making Greyson cackle harder.

"Come on. Don't be such a baby."

I watched them argue. Kalvin had always been stubborn, never wanting anyone to help him. I admired his strength and really looked up to him at times. Greyson was different. I'd only known him for a little bit, but I learned that he went out of his way to help others, even if they were like Kalvin and didn't want his help.

Greyson took a step, reaching for Kalvin's hand, but he pulled it out of Greyson's reach.

Kalvin was easily four inches taller than Greyson, but Greyson seemed to have more muscle. I guessed he would need that for football. Kalvin's muscles were defined. I knew he had a six pack under his cutoff shirt. *Did Greyson have a six pack?* I didn't think I'd seen him shirtless before.

I paused in shock. Comparing the two of them was not something I needed to be doing. I especially didn't need to be thinking about Greyson *shirtless*. I looked around me as though someone might have overheard my thoughts.

Kalvin reluctantly gave Greyson his hand, and he began to heal it. Noah was still practicing the movements Kalvin showed him with the sword.

I exhaled.

No one would have overheard. It was all in my head. I needed to relax.

They continued to bicker. I liked hanging out with them. Feeling anything for either of them would just overcomplicate things. I needed to get my mind back on track to training.

I placed my hand on my hip, ready to step into their

argument with a snarky comment. Just needed to wait for the right moment...

"Elisia!" A familiar stern voice echoed behind me.

My veins turned to ice. I felt stiff as I slowly turned around. My eyes widened. My father, Erlan, stomped towards us.

"Wh-What do you want?"

I wished I hadn't stuttered.

"You are coming home now! You were forbidden from entering Perfidious," he said as he slowed down his strides.

"No."

I willed my body to take a step back, to walk away, to do something. But I couldn't move. I was glued to the spot as my heart beat uncontrollably in my chest.

Erlan's eyes narrowed. "Elisia, you have already worried your mother enough with that silly note you left. You are either an elf or a human. There isn't a place where you can be both."

A small flame sparked inside my chest, thawing some of the ice. "Then where is a place for half-breeds?" my mouth spoke on its own.

"That's not the point, Elisia. Stop misbehaving like one of these stupid mutts."

Monsters called half-breed mutts all the time, but I'd never once remembered my father calling any half-breed such a derogatory name.

He reached out and grabbed my arm.

A lump formed in my throat. I couldn't speak. I couldn't move. I wanted to have a strong face, but Erlan was one monster I didn't think I could win against. I even lost to him in my dream. If I didn't go with him then, it was only a matter of time. He had too many connections. He'd drag me back home eventually.

The flat part of a sword tapped Erlan's elbow. I looked up to see Greyson standing next to me as a pair of hands pulled me back, making Erlan let go of my arm. Kalvin moved me behind him, keeping his arm around me.

"She's not going," Kalvin said, not breaking eye contact with Erlan.

Erlan accessed Greyson, Kalvin, and Noah. He took a step back as his chest puffed out. "Elisia, you better get home after school ends tomorrow, or you will not like the outcome!"

We stood in silence, watching him. I felt tears sting my eyes again, but I didn't want to cry anymore. Not for that man.

Kalvin turned to me. "If he's serious, he'll be able to find ya too easily at my house. We'll have to find somewhere to lay low for a while."

I looked up at Kalvin as Greyson pushed past him and placed his hands on my shoulders. "What the hell was that about?"

I blinked a couple times trying to find the right words. "My father has been corrupted by purebloods. He, um, doesn't like that I'm training you. And as you heard, he doesn't want me in Perfidious anymore."

Greyson's lips parted as he backed away from me.

"I know where we can go. Somewhere no one'll find us." Kalvin's features were tense.

"Do you mean the camp?" I asked.

Kalvin nodded. We hadn't been there since his father died.

"Wait," Greyson waved his hands as if shaking his head

wasn't enough. "What about our training? Someone would be able to follow us when we meet for our lessons."

Kalvin seemed angry, but I couldn't tell why. "It's not close enough for that. It's a day and a half hike north. We're goin' alone."

Noah walked up to the three of us. "But what about school, Elisia? People are gonna wonder where you went."

I shook my head. "I'm not worried about that. We'll only be gone for a little while. Just until things calm down."

An awkward silence filled the air. Greyson's eyes darted back and forth. He made eye contact with Noah before he straightened and looked at me.

"I'm going with you," Greyson stated.

Kalvin clenched his jaw. "Didn't you hear me? We're going alone. You can't come. You have a human life to get back to."

"No, I'm going. It's only for a little while, right? Then, we can keep training, and I can learn more about Perfidious. Like a boot camp. The Elders said that I was your responsibility. Wouldn't it be irresponsible to leave without me?" Greyson smirked.

I glanced at Kalvin. He shrugged and didn't look like he was going to respond.

"He's got a point. We should bring him. I don't want to abandon him." I touched Kalvin's arm, and he relaxed slightly.

Kalvin went to speak, but Noah cut him off. "You wouldn't be leaving until tomorrow, right?"

He nodded.

"Give us the rest of the day off from training," Noah

continued. "Let Greyson think about it. I'm sure he'll change his mind by then."

All I could do was nod before Noah dragged Greyson away. He protested, but Noah gave him a look that made him go along. They grabbed their stuff and started on the path to their house.

20

I grabbed a couple things from the cellar and stepped out to find Kalvin looking me over. He rubbed his chin. I scanned myself before returning my eyes to him.

"Everything okay, Kalvin?" I asked.

"Yup. Let's go. We're gonna go have some fun." Kalvin took the stuff from my arms and grabbed my hand, half dragging me back to his house.

"Kalvin, where are we going?"

He winked at me. "It's a secret."

I rolled my eyes, and he picked up the pace. We jogged to his house and threw our stuff inside. I had no idea where we were headed. As far as I knew, we weren't leaving for the camp until the next day.

Butterflies danced in my stomach. Kalvin was acting strange.

We stopped and got food to go from Shakey's. Then, we started walking on the path going towards Tamara's cave. I didn't know anything down that way other than Tamara's, and there was no way we'd make it all the way there before sunset. I tried asking Kalvin again where we were going, but he refused to answer.

Suddenly, he shot to the left, taking me with him. Off the path, hidden behind elderberry bushes, was a little swing with a board and two strings holding it up. I looked at Kalvin confused. His smile grew.

"Stand on it." He pointed to the swing as he looked up.

I shook my head but did what he asked. His pupils narrowed and he climbed onto the seat beside me.

"Hold on." Kalvin's mischievousness made me wary of what would come next.

He took out his dagger and threw it into the air. My stomach dropped before I realized we were being pulled up into the tree by the swing. I instinctively clung to Kalvin, and laughter vibrated through his chest. The ride was quick, and we soon emerged through a thick section of leaves onto a wooden platform.

My jaw dropped in awe. The platform had little light-bulbs around the top and a couch swing in the middle. The entirety of it was covered by leaves, creating a lush green enclosure. If someone didn't know it was there, they'd never find it.

"What...what is this place?" I asked as I stepped off the wooden board.

"It's where my mom and dad used to meet," Kalvin said as he walked over to a rope hanging on the far side of the platform. He grabbed a hold of it and turned to me. "It's halfway between Coalfell and the mountains. When I was younger, my dad would disappear four nights a week. I didn't find out about it until my mom and I got into a fight."

I nodded, still looking around the place. "I'm guessing that was the big fight about you wanting to live with her?"

Kalvin tilted his head down. "Yup. Well, my dad brought me up here to explain some things, but I really didn't understand why until sunset."

He pulled on the rope, and bright light flooded the platform. I covered my eyes while they adjusted to the brightness.

When I opened them, my breath caught in my lungs.

The platform sat just above the tree line. Purples, pinks, and oranges exploded in the sky beyond like it went on forever. For a moment, I was so struck by its beauty that my mind went blank. I turned back to Kalvin, and his understanding grin brought me back to reality. I relaxed for the first time since the initial fight with my father.

I took a deep breath.

"It's out of this world," I whispered. I was worried if I spoke too loudly, the beauty would get spooked away.

Kalvin motioned for me to sit with him on the swinging couch. He took out the wraps from Shakey's, and I joined him.

"I just wanted ya to relax. You've been so aloof lately." He paused as he looked at the sunset. "This fight with your dad...it wasn't like the rest, was it?"

"No. We disagree *a lot*, but...never like this. It was like he's been forcing me to choose whether I'm a human or an elf. I think he's lost sight that I'm both. Then, he called us mutts and..." I couldn't get the rest of what I was feeling to form into words.

Kalvin gave me a second before talking. "I don't think I've ever seen ya so defeated before. By your expression, I wasn't sure if ya would go with him or fall apart. So, I intervened."

Our eyes met, and I gave him a warm smile. "And I appreciate that. You really are the best." I looked down and picked at my wrap. "I just don't understand what happened with my dad. When he started teaching me to fight, he told me I had the potential to be great. That it didn't matter if I was half-elf because I was all me. But he only trained me for a couple months before he started his job at the castle."

Kalvin nodded. "That was shortly before my dad started trainin' ya."

"Yeah, because my father didn't have time," I said, but then got quiet.

The memories were swirling around my head. I used to have such a good relationship with my father. I didn't understand how things got so bad. I turned back to look at the sunset, my shoulders slumping as I took in the colors. I focused on the beauty in front of me compared to my own thoughts.

I felt Kalvin's eyes glued to me. He really was worried.

My eyes met his. "Can we stay here tonight? It feels so far away from everything."

Kalvin cleared his throat. "No, this place is still here for my mom. I don't want to intrude on it more than I need to. You're welcome to stay at my house again. I don't mind sleeping on the couch." A sad smile appeared on his lips. "I just wish our sleepover didn't involve ya crying yourself to sleep."

I laughed and hit him as I sat up. We gathered the garbage and started walking to the exit. Before we stepped on the wooden board, I pulled Kalvin into a hug.

"Thank you," I whispered.

He put his arm around me and rested his chin on the top of my head.

"Anytime," he replied.

We walked the entire way back to his house without a word. We both knew that words weren't needed. We were the best of friends, and sometimes talking wasn't necessary. Just having Kalvin there was enough to brighten my world again.

I stumbled backwards a couple steps and stopped, a tree at my back. I could feel the injuries becoming real as I leaned against the tree. I kept eyeing the creature in front of me. His yellow eyes were lifeless, but that didn't mean he was dead. I began to get my breathing under control to calm myself down and hissed in pain as the adrenaline started to leave my body. I heard a rustle come from behind me and quickly moved to put myself in between my friends and the noise. I unsheathed my Tonfas and felt my body pulse with pain.

I gasped and tried to sit up, but someone had me by the shoulders. I struggled against him until the sunlight from the window caught his face. Black, bedhead hair cascaded around his face as he stared at me with wide eyes. Kalvin slowly removed his hands from my shoulders as I sat up, holding my head.

I closed my eyes to relax myself, trying to force my mind to put the dream away, but it was getting harder with every realistic nightmare. Eventually, my breathing slowed to normal.

"Ya okay?" Kalvin asked next to me.

I turned around to look at the sleepy half-breed. I didn't want to talk about it.

"Weren't you on the couch a few hours ago?" I asked, ignoring his question.

Kalvin sighed and tilted his head. "Yes...but it sounded like ya were havin' a nightmare in here. Are you okay?" Kalvin emphasized the last question since I didn't answer him the first time.

I shivered at the thought of the dream and forced a smile. "Yeah, I'll be fine. Just a bad dream."

Kalvin frowned as he got out of the bed and headed out of the bedroom.

Someone knocked.

I got out of the bed myself. I had to dawdle since my muscles were weak from my nightmare and the room was spinning slightly. By the time I got to the bedroom door, I heard Greyson's voice.

"Good. You're still here. Sorry to just barge in like this," Greyson said, entering the house.

Confused, I walked around to the front door. Greyson and Noah walked in with backpacks and a duffle bag. Greyson's eyes met mine and went emotionless.

"Oh, you're here too. I thought...you'd be..." Greyson shook his head.

Noah spoke up. "We talked to my parents. We forged a football camp acceptance letter. Should buy us about a week. Let's go to that place you were talking about, Kalvin."

"Seriously?" Kalvin wasn't awake yet and hadn't had time to think. His eyes were barely open, and I could tell he was trying so hard to follow the events going on.

"Yes. When are we leaving?"

"Do I have to explain how dangerous it is for Noah to go?" I asked, too tired to bicker.

Greyson scratched the back of his head. "About that..."

Noah gave me a smug grin. "I'm going. I know which direction you're headed, approximately how long it will take, and from that I can figure out a rough area of where the camp is. And I can tell your dad."

Kalvin grunted as he glanced sideways at me. "We could always kill him."

Noah's smile faltered.

"Hm. It would cause too much attention." I sighed. "I don't think we can."

Kalvin ran his hand down his face and cursed under his breath. He turned back to me. "Fine. You're right. We can gather supplies and head out shortly after. By the time Erlan comes looking for us, we'll be long gone."

The thought of my father not being able to find me made me happy. "We'll need to take something to cover our scent and mask Noah's."

"Yup, Jasper should have something." Kalvin walked back into his room, changed, and came back out. "I'll go see if he's awake. Ya get the bags ready."

Kalvin left, and I snickered. Both Greyson and Noah looked at me as they set their bags down.

"He won't be back for at least an hour," I explained. "Jasper and Kalvin never stop talking when they're together."

"We packed a good amount of stuff," Noah, changing the subject quickly. "We filled the duffle with non-perishables and camping stuff that my parents won't miss."

He opened up the duffle so I could see what was inside.

"Okay, that's great." I saw food that just needed hot water, like instant pastas. "So, we'll all carry a backpack filled with some food, clothes, a blanket, and the essentials, just so one of us can survive if we get separated. Which shouldn't happen, but just in case." I opened up Kalvin's closet and found some extra blankets.

Noah started to rearrange his bags. I grabbed some backpacks out of a different closet and set it all down next to Noah. I scanned the supplies out in front of me, but Greyson cleared his throat, catching my attention. I turned around to look at him.

"Elisia, can I talk to you, um, outside?" Greyson asked. He seemed upset about something, but I didn't know what it could be.

I nodded as I followed him and left Noah to work on the bags. Greyson closed the door behind us and faced me.

His face fell as he put his hand on my shoulder. "What's going on, Elisia? Are you okay?"

Did Kalvin tell him something?

"What do you mean?" I tried to act casual.

"Yesterday, you showed up late, and you came from the village. Then, your father showed up threatening to take you away. Now today, you're at Kalvin's house. Why wouldn't you just stay at your place?" Greyson asked.

"I'm sorry, Greyson. It's just been an emotional weekend, and I didn't want to talk about it," I said, not feeling especially fond of being questioned.

His shoulders slumped. "I just...I want to know what's going on. I don't want you to be downplaying it at all. If you're not okay, I need to know."

"Greyson, I told you the basics yesterday. I don't want to go into the details," I repeated, sounding harsher than I meant to, but it wasn't easy talking about it. I just wished he understood that.

Greyson sighed. "That's not what I meant." His words were soft as he spoke to me. "I'm here too, though. You know that, right?"

I curled the side of my lips in a half smile, nodding. It wasn't that he was trying to force it out of me. He wanted me to know that I wasn't alone, probably the same way that I did for him after he found out all of the monster stuff. I probably should have apologized, but I didn't know if I wanted to. I'd talk to him later. It was still too fresh.

I led him back into the house. Noah had all the food lined up on the table and the clothes they brought in two backpacks. I grabbed a backpack for me and started putting the clothes from my duffle into the backpack. Kalvin had some clothes set out, so I shoved them into another backpack.

An hour later, we had everything we needed to get to the camp. From there, we could get more supplies from the camp or the village nearby. I carried Kalvin's backpack along with my own as we started to walk over to Jasper's place.

21

We got to Jasper's house located closer to town. It looked the same as Kalvin's on the outside, except for the multitude of plants lining the walkway and crawling up the sides of the cabin. Many of the plants had special properties that Jasper made his powders from, such as healing, gardening, and concealing scent.

I entered the open front door and immediately heard the irritation in Jasper's voice. "No, Kalvin, for the fifth time. That's too much. You'll run out of powder before you get to your destination."

"Sure. I'll do as you say," Kalvin responded absent-mindedly.

"You moron. I can see your soul. I know you're lying." Jasper's back was to us as we walked into the room. He turned around and faked surprise to see me. His white hair swirled around his head with the sudden movement. "Look who decided to grace us with her glorious presence."

His eyes were pitch black as they looked into mine. Then, the iris of his eye turned green.

"Oh, darling!" Jasper rushed over to me and took my hand. "That pain is not how a splendid elf like you should be feeling. Let me ease it, won't you?"

"No, but thank you, Jasper. I appreciate the thought." I took back my hand. His eyes turned back to black.

Jasper looked behind me with his childish grin. "Hm, who are these new faces? I don't believe I've seen them around before."

I pointed to them. "This is Greyson and Noah. They are—"

Jasper suddenly dropped to one knee and bowed his head in reverence. Greyson looked awkward and uncomfortable.

"Come on, man!" Kalvin said, running a hand down his face.

Jasper stood up. "If you would allow me the honor, I would love to join your army, King's Heir." Jasper bowed his head again.

"Uh..." Greyson glanced at Noah, a slight grin on his face. "Sure? Why not?" Greyson shrugged at the question. He looked around at all of us and cocked his head as he turned his attention back to Jasper. "How do you know who I am?"

Kalvin put his arm on Jasper's shoulder and pulled him away from Greyson. "I told him, hoping he'd give me the stuff we needed for free. But all he gave me was an attitude and a crappy discount."

"And you should be grateful." Jasper said, looking disappointed. "The powder has ingredients that are scarce and hard to get a hold of."

"I also told him not to be weird, but he didn't listen," Kalvin said, glaring at Jasper.

Jasper's eyes turned a light blue, his face brightening. "Sorry, I just can't believe it. Everyone has been waiting for so long. No one even knew if an heir would appear after all this time. But look, he's finally here."

I watched Jasper. I didn't always trust him. I could never tell what his eye color meant, and I knew he wanted to keep it that way.

"Okay, well, we'll be leaving then." Kalvin said, walking to my side.

I handed him his backpack, and he threw it over one shoulder.

"I'll see you around. Hopefully, you bring Elisia next time you're cranky and half awake. She really is your better half." Jasper said, looking at Kalvin with purple eyes. Then, he bowed his head to Greyson. "King's Heir, I will spread the word of your return, but don't worry. I will keep it underground so the Council doesn't catch on."

Greyson nodded.

I wanted to push him out, but Noah beat me to it. He put Greyson in front of him and smiled at Jasper.

Greyson started walking next to me once we got far enough away from Jasper's place. "So, what is Jasper? I haven't read anything that can change eye color like that."

"He's a whisper," I answered and turned to look at Noah. "Have you read about them yet?"

Noah nodded. "A whisper is a creature that can read and manipulate souls. The book said they are known to be guides. They like helping people within their communities. They prefer to be alone, apart from any other whispers. I can't remember why though."

It surprised me that Noah learned so much after just over a week. His brow creased as he looked at me.

"It didn't say anything about their eye color changing. What do the colors mean?"

Kalvin answered him. "No one really knows. They don't tell anyone. The only thing Jasper has told me is that his eyes are black when he's not using his powers. He usually just uses them to read people. He's eccentric, but he's harmless."

"I don't trust these monsters." Noah kicked some rocks and didn't make eye contact with any of us. "So many of them could benefit from Greyson becoming the king. I just think they're gonna either use him or want him dead, right? There's no in-between."

I looked over at Noah with a raised eyebrow. It didn't occur to me that Noah's distrust of monsters would be a good thing. It was probably the reason that the Elders wanted us to train him with Greyson. I grew up around monsters and half-breeds, so I had learned to trust certain breeds, but who knows if even they would be trustworthy in a situation like that.

The king's bloodline returning was going to change everything.

22

W e would have to walk about thirty-five miles to the camp, and it seemed to take forever. *Would Greyson and Noah be able to handle that long of a trip?*

From what I could remember, the way there was mostly safe. I didn't remember running into any monsters when we were with Aaron, but he also marked a path specifically to avoid any villages or known monster dens. We hadn't gone that way in so long. It could have changed since then. Hopefully, it hadn't.

I looked around while we walked during the morning hours, tracking the sun so I knew the approximate time. It was just before noon. That was something Kalvin's father had taught me, and it always came in handy.

But no matter how many times I walked through those woods, I would never get used to the beauty I saw. The path was different compared to the normal green plants, bushes, and occasional flower patches. Heading along the flatlands, more meadows and clearings with blue and white flowers peaked around the corners.

We came up to a group of moss-covered trees. A black line marked our path, a remnant of Kalvin's father. Aaron had taken a can of spray paint to all the trees along the way to the camp. It was enough for someone to follow, but not too much for others to notice if they didn't know what it was.

By the time the sun passed its peak, everyone was more talkative. Noah wanted to learn more about the different monsters that still existed. So I was helping him go through a book he brought with him from Antheia's bookstore.

Suddenly, Kalvin started snickering.

"I know I'm not the best at explaining stuff, but do you have to laugh at me?" I asked him as he stopped walking to look at something.

"That tree." Kalvin nudged me.

He pointed up ahead. It had a thick trunk with a log in front of it. Halfway up, it split into three separate branches.

I smiled warmly at him and chuckled.

"What about it?" Greyson asked.

I looked away from Kalvin to see Greyson scanning the tree, probably wondering why it was special.

"Sorry, I completely forgot," I said in between giggles. "That's where Kalvin and I first met."

I felt bad that I forgot about it. It happened so long ago. I told them about how Kalvin and I met there—how he looked strange to me, and how he didn't like the way I smelled.

"I was so mad at him," I said, finishing my story.

Greyson and Noah were both cracking up.

Kalvin protested. "What'd I do to upset ya so much?"

I grinned at the memory again as I put my hands on my hips, trying to look annoyed. "You said I smelled weird."

He threw his hands up like he surrendered. "Ya did when I was younger. Ya were the first elf half-breed I met, and at that time, I didn't like the way ya smelled."

I walked in front of him so he would have to look me in the eyes.

"And now?" I raised an eyebrow, curious to see how he would respond.

"Oh..." Noah yelled into the air. "Kalvin, I'd be careful. You're in dangerous territory here."

Kalvin realized what he said and looked mildly concerned. "Now, you smell like Elisia. You don't smell weird to me anymore."

I huffed and crossed my arms.

He smirked and leaned closer to me. His warmth radiated from him in waves. Kalvin sniffed the air near my neck. His velvet voice reached my ear.

"You smell similar to vanilla."

The moment was no longer than a second, but my heart was racing. I tried to hide my nerves by laughing.

Greyson sniffed the air in my direction. "It's more like a spicy vanilla."

My jaw dropped while everyone laughed.

"What do I smell like?" Greyson asked Kalvin excitedly.

"You smell..." I pretended to sniff the air like they did. "Like a dork."

Already several hours into the hike, we stopped for lunch. Everyone continued to joke about smells, and all seemed content. There weren't any Elders to worry about, no parents, no problems relevant at that moment. At least my life was getting back to normal—or as normal as it could be being a half-breed.

We continued on the trail after packing up the bags. Kalvin changed the subject to fighting techniques. He showed them different movements and told them to repeat. Kalvin had me show them how to defend against it so they learned both offense and defense.

Even though we were talking about training, we were relaxed. No one needed to worry about anything real. There would be plenty of time for that later. The trip was probably good for all of us to step away from the big serious topics and just focus on the present.

That night we stopped in an open area in the woods. Because of Noah being human, we had to take it slower than planned. The day and a half hike might turn into two full days or more, but that didn't seem to bother anyone. We set up camp a little way off the trail so that anyone who walked by wouldn't find us.

Greyson healed the minor cuts and bruises from the sparring before dinner. We ate and started getting the blankets out, setting up the camp so that we could go to sleep.

"I'll take the first watch," I said before Kalvin could.

He needed his rest, especially since I woke him up the night before with my nightmare.

I started to climb a tree so no one could protest and sat on one of the lower branches, watching as everyone got settled. The horizon darkened, reminding me of the sunset Kalvin showed me. The thought flushed me with warmth.

Halfway through the night, Kalvin woke up and

insisted I get some rest. I wanted to protest, but he gave me a look that told me to shut up and accept his offer. Leaving the blanket on the branch, I crawled down and laid in the dirt where he was sleeping. I watched Kalvin climb up the tree, but I didn't remember seeing him make it to the branch. I fell asleep before I could.

23

The sun woke me up as it peeked over the trees. I looked around to see that the other two boys were still sleeping. I got up and started to pack away my things, wanting to be ready to leave or help others pack their stuff up after breakfast.

About an hour later, everyone was sitting around the fire, but not everyone was really awake. We ate some pasta and really wished we'd brought coffee. I was used to getting up in the morning, but I never woke up quickly. Kalvin seemed tired but not like the rest of us.

It would be another long day of walking, yet it was exciting to think about. I hadn't gone on that long of a trip with Greyson or Noah. Maybe it would give me the chance to get to know them better.

Once we were walking again, I made sure to walk next to Greyson. I had a question I was curious about.

"So, Greyson, what would you have done if you didn't find out what your birthmark meant?"

"Um, I'm not sure. I was thinking about going into the

medical field in college and getting into genetics. I thought maybe I could find answers through that and see if my birthmark was some sort of genetic mutation." He smiled at me. "Like that would have really done any good."

I looked at my hands. "Yeah, I never really thought about the differences of human genes versus elf or dragon genes. You probably would have found out you weren't human."

"Hm," Greyson frowned as his eyes glazed over in thought. "That'd be interesting to explore. I do like the medical field. Science and history were always my favorite subjects, but I don't exactly have the best grades to get into a good pre-med school. Noah's the book smart one. Not me."

"You could always talk to Ms. Needham about it. I'm sure she's done some research, and she could probably help you get into a school. She is a human/monster doctor," I suggested.

Noah jogged up next to him. "As long as we still get to go to colleges on the same coast. Right, Greyson?"

Greyson looked at me and smirked. "That *was* the plan."

But it seemed like there was more in that statement than Greyson was willing to say out loud.

"I got accepted to all the great Business schools: Stanford, Columbia, UPenn. Greyson is still waiting on his acceptance letters," Noah bragged. "We were doing research right before all this happened. We'll have to get back to that when we go home."

"Sure." Greyson obviously didn't share Noah's excitement.

I decided to change the subject. I jogged up to Kalvin and grabbed his arm. "How about we play Bobcat?"

"What's that?" Noah asked curiously.

"It's technically a human game. In the human version, people walk on a trail and when someone yells 'Bobcat', everyone has to either climb onto a tree or just hang onto the trunk, as long as you're not touching the ground," Kalvin explained. "But my father made up a different version after we took Elisia to the camp for the first time so that we had something to do while we were traveling. In his version, there is one 'Bobcat'. That person hides in the bushes or trees; any abilities or weapons are free game— even wings. They attack someone walking with them. They only get one chance to attack before someone else gets to a turn to be the 'Bobcat'."

A rush of giddiness filled me. "But no one yells 'Bobcat' in his version. The 'Bobcat' just attacks without warning. It's to practice sneak attacks and defending against them. I learned quickly to not attack Aaron. He was human, but damn...He was so in tune to everything going on around him, I didn't even make it within arm's reach before he stopped me. And that's with my elf abilities," I said.

A spark flickered in Noah's eyes.

"Sounds like fun," Greyson said. "Who wants to be the 'Bobcat' first?"

I was about to say I would, but I never got the chance.

My instincts sent a spark through my stomach. I reached for my Tonfa blades at my sides, but I wasn't fast enough. The earth exploded under my feet, and something scaly threw me into the air.

Greyson sprouted wings and flew towards me, catching

me midair. Below us, the green and yellow scales of a snake slithered out of the ground.

I scanned the area for Kalvin and Noah, worried about where they ended up. I spotted Kalvin ducking from bush to bush just out of sight of the snake.

"Greyson," I asked above the noise of his wings, "where's Noah?"

It took him a second to answer, but I felt his chest expand with relief on my back. "Over by the tail. It looks like he got knocked back by the snake."

I saw Noah exactly where Greyson said. He was getting up slowly, reaching for his sword that was sticking out of the top of his bag. He seemed terrified and unsure, but before I could get to him, something blocked my path. The snake spotted us and was about to strike at the air.

"Drop me and fly up!" I yelled at Greyson.

He hesitated.

"Now!" I yelled, and he immediately released me.

I fell to the earth as Greyson shot up into the sky.

The snake barely missed us. Another second and it would not have ended well. My feet slammed into the ground, and I rolled, trying to get a grip on the earth. I pulled my own weapons out of their sheaths, swinging them into place.

The snake was ready to attack again.

I threw my body to the left as the snake snapped at me, taking a mouthful of dirt and grass. I didn't have time to recover. The snake swung its head, hitting me in the center of my body, forcing the wind from my lungs. I flew back several feet, landing on my back.

The snake flailed around like it was in pain. I moved, ignoring my sore body, to see its other side and saw Kalvin hanging on to one of the daggers wedged between the snake's scales.

I was about to run in front of the creature, but I decided against it. With the way the monster was moving, it could easily smash me. I quickly placed my Tonfas in their sheaths as I ran for the body. The snake was only about five feet in diameter and probably forty feet long. I jumped over and slid down the other side.

Metal flashed as a sword came down at my head.

"Hey!" I exclaimed as I dropped and rolled away from the attacker.

Noah struck the snake, sinking into the skin a few inches. I didn't have time to think. I went to grab Noah before the snake came for the two of us.

Red wings filled my vision before Noah was carried into the sky by Greyson. A little shocked, I turned and pulled the sword from the snake's skin. The head of the snake came towards me.

I put the sword up to protect myself, but instead of hitting me, he slithered past me. I kept focused on the head to keep its mouth away from me, not seeing any sense in the snake's movements.

I realized what it was doing too late.

The snake curled around me and squeezed. The blade of the sword pulled against me and the side of it dug into my shoulder. I hissed in pain as I searched frantically for some way out. Two beady eyes came closer, looking into my own.

The snake opened its mouth.

I closed my eyes for what would happen next.

The pressure suddenly released around me as Kalvin stabbed the snake's eye. I held onto my shoulder as I climbed out of the snake's body, but Kalvin was thrown back.

"Hey, ugly! Over here!" Noah yelled waving his arms. I looked back to the snake to see if Kalvin was still there.

He wasn't.

"You barely know how to fight!" Kalvin yelled. I turned around to see him running from the trees. "Let us take care of it!"

Greyson swooped down in front of him. "No. Go to the left." Greyson handed Kalvin his sword. "Elisia, to the right. The easiest way to kill it is to decapitate it. I'll hold the head down. You'll only have a few seconds."

Greyson took off into the air without letting either of us protest. I knew I didn't have time to disagree and ran into position. Noah ran around like he was trying to play the most dangerous game of football I'd ever seen. But Noah wouldn't last too long. He was fast, but he was only human.

Greyson came down on the snake's head like a meteor. The entire snake went limp. Seeing my opening, I immediately went in. I took Noah's sword in my hand and was ready to bring it down. For a split second, I looked up and saw Kalvin bringing down the sword on the other side. We both made contact at the same time, dragging our blades through the neck until we hit the ground. Dark red blood splattered Kalvin and me from the decapitated beast. We stayed alert as we slowly removed our blades and backed away. The rest of the body was still wiggling around, but the head remained still.

We won.

I stood up, ambling. I felt like if I moved too fast, I would wake it up, and we would have to start all over. My body shook from the adrenaline pumping through my veins. My breath came in short, skittish breaths. I couldn't get enough air into my lungs.

I looked around at everyone. Noah had the biggest smile on his face from winning his first fight. Greyson was still looking around, moving slow like I was. Then my gaze met Kalvin's.

"Let's go." Kalvin said.

I nodded.

I used my speed to run as fast as I could. I grabbed Noah's and Greyson's backpacks as Kalvin grabbed his and mine. I ran over to the stunned pair of guys and handed them the bags.

"Greyson, fly. Carry Noah. Stay over us," I ordered.

He opened his mouth to speak, but we didn't have time.

"I'll explain later. Move. Now!"

Kalvin threw me my bag from behind as we started to run.

We needed to get away from the snake as fast as possible. The blood would attract other dangerous monsters, and I didn't think we could go against anything else. At least the dead snake would be enough of a distraction to keep other monsters away from us.

Greyson and Noah weren't very good at fighting yet. We won, but we got in each other's way during the fight. I didn't know if it was because we hadn't gotten to know each other's styles or if there was some other reason.

With the fight over, we just needed to get out of there.

King Lawrence proposed to Miranda on April 4th, 1869. He feared what trouble it would cause but continued with the wedding preparations. He didn't want to rule alone like the Shapeshifter King before him. It seemed everything had become peaceful again by Miranda's coronation in 1895.

In 1914, after the announcement of Miranda's pregnancy, the threats and attempts on King Lawrence's life increased. He realized that he was no longer a beloved king. But that didn't change the way he ruled.

King Lawrence believed half-breeds and purebloods shouldn't be treated differently. Having so many species in Perfidious, it was only a matter of time before there would be more half-breeds than purebloods, and many purebloods saw a betrayal in his decision to bear an heir with Miranda.

Unbeknownst to the king and his wife, a group of pureblood monsters started an organization to remove King Lawrence, whom they began calling the "Impure King."

An excerpt from The King's Legacy:
A Complete History of Perfidious

24

We ran for about two to three miles before Kalvin led the way to a pond. The water came into view, and I started to slow down, eager to catch my breath.

Greyson set Noah down near Kalvin and me, but he didn't land—he went back into the air.

"Greyson! What are you doing?" I yelled.

He ignored me and continued to fly away until he was out of sight.

"Greyson! Stay here!" I turned to the other two, grabbing a hold of a low branch. "I'll go get him."

I left Kalvin and Noah as I started to climb the tree. My shoulder pulsed with pain. I had to scale with only one hand, which took me longer than usual, but I continued until I could see over the top of the other tree.

The branches were thinner and couldn't support my weight. I had to stop. I looked around for Greyson and finally saw him flying back.

I yelled his name to get his attention. "Greyson!"

He saw me and flew over, hovering in the air a few feet away from me.

"What are you doing?" I asked, scanning him for injuries. Thankfully, I couldn't see any.

"I wanted to make sure the snake was dead. I didn't want it following us."

"Fine," I sighed.

Greyson reached out and wrapped his arms around my waist. The stress melted from my body as I relaxed into him. His green eyes never left mine. He lifted me from the branch and slowly descended from the sky. Our feet touched the ground, but neither one of us moved. There was something in his eyes that I couldn't look away from. It was like he wanted to say something but couldn't find the words. Or he was sad, maybe unsure about something. I couldn't figure it out. I parted my lips to ask him if everything was okay.

But before I could, he blinked several times and took a step back. The warmth from his embrace left me.

I turned to check on the others to distract myself from what just happened. Kalvin was making sure Noah's minimal injuries weren't too serious. Noah was a little beat up, but nothing more than a few bruises and scrapes. Kalvin looked okay too—mostly just covered in dirt and snake blood.

"Elisia?" Greyson said behind me.

He was looking at the blood that stained his clothes from his chest to his abdomen. His eyes were wide as he stared at me. I followed his concerned gaze to my chest.

The blood on him was mine.

Greyson walked over to me and placed his hand on my cut without hesitation. His hand gently pressed onto the front of my shoulder. A green light glistened as he trailed the line of blood down my shirt, making my skin hot where he touched. He held his hand there a second after the green shimmer vanished, moving his eyes to mine. They were fighting to not show any sign of weakness, but I could tell it took a lot out of him to heal me.

He removed his hand, leaving only a rip in my t-shirt and snake blood.

"Thanks, but it wasn't a major cut. I would've been fine." I told him.

"That won't stop me from taking care of you," he said before he walked over to help Noah.

Kalvin backed away from the group and started walking into the pond. I followed his lead. The water was cool, but after a second, it felt warm. I slowly sunk in. Silence consumed me as I sank underwater, wiping blood from my face and hair. Needing air, I surfaced.

A splash of water smacked my cheek.

Kalvin smirked.

Noah cannonballed into the water followed by Greyson, turning the tiny pond into a monsoon. I washed off the blood as much as possible before I got out, leaving the boys to their splashing war.

I dug through my bag to see if I could use my blanket, but I couldn't find it. It must have fallen out during all the commotion. I grabbed a dirty shirt to use as a towel. Hidden from the boys' view, I changed into dry clothes and hung the wet stuff to dry. A fire was my next priority. I didn't even want to think about how cold it would get overnight.

I looked up at the sky. We only had about an hour

before dusk, and I didn't think we'd be able to make it to the camp before then.

Water sprinkled me from behind. I shrieked, turning around to see Kalvin shaking like a dog with a huge grin on his face.

"Oh, sorry, did I get you wet?" he asked me, unable to hold back a snicker.

"You jerk," I yelled back at him, but I couldn't help laughing.

"Hey guys!" Noah called from the pond.

We looked over to see Noah supporting Greyson to walk. He looked like he could barely stand up on his own.

I ran over and wrapped his other arm around my shoulders. Greyson tensed up at my sudden closeness but quickly relaxed and smiled down at me weakly. We walked him over to the fire and sat him down, wrapping a blanket around him.

Kalvin squatted down next to me and scanned him. "Were ya injured or bit anywhere?"

Greyson shook his head. "No, I'll be okay. I think I overdid it by shifting and healing the two of them. The weakness just kinda hit me. I need rest, and I'll be good to go."

Kalvin shook his head. "Ya need to not overdo it. Your body only has so much energy. Even though you're gaining stamina by using your abilities, ya can only do so much. At some point, ya won't have any energy left, and if ya lose it all. That's it, you're dead."

Kalvin paused, letting the information sink in. He didn't continue until after Greyson nodded.

"Ya need time to let your body rest and recover. We'll

make camp here and travel the rest of the distance tomorrow."

The boys all changed while I grabbed more firewood. I got back, finding clothes and blankets hanging from branches around the fire. It didn't take us long to grab food and crowd around the warmth.

"I'll take first watch," Kalvin said, probably knowing I would have.

"I'll take the second. Wake me up when you get tired, okay?" I told him.

I looked away but saw Kalvin elbow Noah out of the corner of my eye.

"Oh, right. I already told Kalvin I'd take the second watch." Noah shrugged.

I gave Kalvin a look as Noah continued sorting through his bag and talking to Greyson.

He came up to me and whispered so the others wouldn't hear. "You've barely gotten any sleep the last three nights. Don't fight me on this. You need your beauty rest." He winked at me.

I knew I needed sleep. I was exhausted, so I had no plans to argue with him.

Kalvin grabbed his blanket and found a good spot in a tree. Greyson and Noah were still talking as I laid down in the dirt closest to the fire, hoping to get some sleep. Even though it was cold, I easily fell asleep without a blanket.

Greyson hovered in the air in front of me. He gripped his sword tightly as he breathed hard. A harpy girl flew opposite of him, using her claw-like hands for weapons. Feathers covered her body, some even blended in with her dark brown, almost black hair. She came at him like a cat playing with her food. Something wasn't right.

They were speaking, but I couldn't hear what they were saying. Her eyes were cold. He dodged her attack and flew behind her. He panted as she yelled at him.

In one swift movement, she smacked his sword out of his hands. She flipped around and brought her clawed leg down on his chest. Greyson dropped like a bird that got shot out of the sky.

My eyes shot open. I sat up, my eyes immediately searching for Greyson. He was asleep, curled up with a wing around his body, laying near my feet by the fire.

It was just a dream.

I looked down. Someone had put a blanket on me.

I got up slowly, suddenly so dizzy that it was hard to stand. I managed to make it over to Greyson and draped the blanket over him. It was my fault that I didn't have one. I didn't want to use someone else's.

He stirred.

"No, Elisia," Greyson said sleepily. "You were shivering. You need it."

"Stop being stubborn. I'm not gonna take it from you." I watched as his wing disappeared. I went to stand up, but he grabbed my wrist and pulled me down beside him. He arranged the blanket so it would cover both of us.

"You need to be warm too." He turned his back to me and went to sleep.

I pulled the blanket up to my neck and shook my head. I was too tired to argue. Being close to him after that dream relaxed me, and I quickly fell back asleep.

25

I woke up with the blanket all to myself. Greyson was packing up and putting out the fire. I quickly started gathering up my things.

"Morning, sleeping beauty." Kalvin said, kneeling down next to me. He was smiling, but something seemed off. "Did you sleep well?"

"Yeah. I guess so. Are we ready to go?" I asked, grabbing Kalvin's hand to help me stand.

"Almost. We are only about five miles from camp. We'll eat there. If I remember correctly, there's food stored there and a market about a mile east of the camp. We'll be able to stock up on supplies at some point. We're runnin' pretty low." Kalvin hesitated. "We also have a problem."

He held up an empty bag with a fancy "J" on it and shrugged.

"We ran out of the powder to cover our scents, but we're so close. I don't think five miles'll matter. Noah still has enough to hide his scent."

I raised an eyebrow and couldn't hide my giggle. "Didn't Jasper say something about not using too much?" I asked him matter-of-factly.

He waved his hand in a dismissive fashion. "Yea, yea. Save the 'I told ya so.' I'll hear it from Jasper when he hears about it."

We started walking as soon as we put everything into our bags. I looked over at Greyson, who seemed to be avoiding me. He wouldn't look at me, and I didn't know why.

Did I do something?

We walked in an awkward silence for the next couple of miles. It became clear that something was bothering Greyson. I grabbed his arm, pulling him away from Kalvin and Noah. I knew Noah wouldn't be able to hear us, and I was hoping Kalvin would get the hint I didn't want him listening.

"What's with you?" I asked him.

He kept his eyes looking straight ahead. "Nothing's wrong."

"Bullshit. You won't even look at me." I pulled on his arm to get him to look at me, but he stopped walking instead.

Greyson waited for a moment. His eyes watched Kalvin and Noah walk farther away. When he seemed content with how far they were, he finally faced me, keeping his eyes on the ground. His cheeks were pink. "It's because of last night. I was half asleep and didn't mean to pull you under the blanket with me. You just looked cold, and I didn't think about it. I just acted."

I couldn't help but chuckle. "That's what this is about?"

Greyson nodded with flushed cheeks and scratched the back of his head.

"Don't worry about it, Greyson," I tried to tell him casually, but on the inside my heart was racing. Could he hear it? "You shared the blanket with me. It wasn't like you cuddled up to me or anything. As far as I remember, we slept back-to-back. Relax, okay? It's not anything to be embarrassed about."

Greyson nodded and started walking again. His pace was quick so we could catch up to the others, but he still seemed tense. I increased my pace until I was a little in front of him and dropped my body, swinging my leg to smack his ankles. His legs flew out from under him.

I stuck out my tongue. He looked at me wide-eyed.

"You shouldn't avoid someone who can kick your ass."

Some of the tension melted from his body. His muscular arms lifted him up, and he showed me his normal, charming grin.

"I'll get you back one of these days," Greyson joked as we caught up to the others.

"Hey, Greyson." Noah tried to hold in his snicker. "Have a nice trip?"

Everyone burst into laughter.

I watched Kalvin and Noah tease Greyson, trying to ignore the thoughts running through my head. But it was hard. The memory of Greyson half asleep, trying to make sure I was warm, played over and over again in my head.

I wanted it to stop.

I didn't want to get my hopes up that Greyson might have feelings for me. Greyson couldn't like me. We were just friends, like Kalvin and me. He was probably just embarrassed because I was a girl.

Did he have much experience with girls?

A lot of girls swooned over him at school, but did he really date any of them? I couldn't remember him ever having a girlfriend. A smile rose to my lips. Then, I shook it off.

No.

I wasn't allowed to think like that. There were other more important things to worry about, like all the stuff with the king's heir. I didn't need to worry about boys. I needed to stay focused.

We reached the camp about an hour later, passing a large fence on our way through the gate. Inside the fence, there were three different buildings: two with bunks, the other smaller and meant for storage. We checked the buildings before settling down. Noah and Greyson checked on the storage building while Kalvin and I checked out the bunk houses.

The first one seemed to be good, but I kept getting a strange feeling. "Kalvin, do you feel that?"

Kalvin's orange eyes scanned the room.

He nodded as we walked towards the second building. We opened the door, finding the room much darker than it should have been. I couldn't see anything inside. The only light came from the door, but the shadows seemed too dark and too thick to be natural.

Kalvin and I barely had time to move before a dagger shot out of the darkness. I watched in slow motion as the dagger grazed Kalvin's cheek, slicing through his dragon skin. We both jumped back and waited for whoever—or whatever—was hiding to make the next move.

A female voice came from inside. "That was a warning shot. Who are you and why are you here?"

I scanned the surroundings, not sure if others were around. "It doesn't matter who we are. This is his father's camp. Who are *you* and why are *you* here?"

The darkness in the building started to dim as a girl took form, stepping into the light. Her skin was light brown, and her hair was dark black.

"Name's Keira. I found this place abandoned." Keira licked her lips as her eyes darted nervously between the two of us. "I've been staying here for a couple weeks while things cool down in my village. I didn't mean to trespass." She held her hands up as she slowly walked down the steps of the cabin, weapons strapped to her sides. "I mean you no harm. I know I'm outnumbered, and I will see myself out."

"You said your name is Keira?" Greyson asked, coming up behind me and putting away his weapon.

She nodded.

"We have come here for the same reason. There are some things back home that we wanted to get away from. Since we are in the same boat, I don't mind sharing the camp. It is plenty big enough." Greyson straightened out of his defensive stance and started to approach her. He looked her straight in the eyes and took slow long strides.

I grabbed his arm as he passed by me.

"What are you doing? That's not your decision," I whispered harshly.

"Nothing good is gonna come from kicking her out," Greyson whispered back.

"And what do we do if we have her stay?" Kalvin asked.

"I don't know! But she's in the same situation as we are. Why can't we let her stay?" Greyson countered, pointing over to her.

Keira tapped her foot, her hands still in the air. She was definitely showing she meant no harm and wasn't making a move to stay. Maybe we could coexist with her.

I let go of Greyson. He turned towards Keira. Her posture straightened as she waited for us to speak.

"Do ya have anywhere else to go?" Kalvin asked.

Keira huffed. "Pff, of course I don't. I wouldn't be in the middle of nowhere if I did."

"Would ya like to stay?" Kalvin asked.

She opened her mouth to speak but closed it as her eyes softened. She nodded.

Kalvin glanced at me. "Fine. We'll have to figure out sleeping arrangements."

Keira's eyes scanned all of us as she lowered her hands. She was obviously very distrusting of the situation.

As was I.

Greyson held out his hand. "My name's Greyson. That's Elisia, Noah, and Kalvin."

Keira's shoulders relaxed as she hesitantly shook Greyson's hand.

Noah joined Greyson and Keira. "What are you? You look so human. You're a half-breed, right?"

"I'm a shadow, and I *know* you're human. No one—pureblood or half-breed—would be so bold to ask a question like that."

Keira quickly turned around and went back into the cabin.

There was something about her I didn't trust. It wasn't like we knew anything about her.

I wanted to tell Greyson that he was wrong, that it was a bad idea, but my gut said to stay quiet and see what she was up to. Who knows, maybe she'd make a good ally? But I couldn't just give her the benefit of the doubt with so much on the line.

What would she do if she found out who Greyson really was?

26

We went to work settling at the camp. I checked the firewood and went to get more. I returned to find Noah preparing dinner while taking inventory of what we had brought along with what was left in the storage room.

I looked around the camp and saw Kalvin. He glanced at me briefly before looking back to Keira.

"Hey," I said sitting down next to him. "Something up?"

"Just strange to see a shadow all by herself. Usually they're a pack species." Kalvin turned to me and shook his head. He was still frowning and ran his hand down his face. "Sorry. No, nothing's up. Did you need something?"

"Do you know where Greyson is? I don't see him."

"Well, he was here earlier. He might have gone to check out the surroundings. I think I saw him heading out the gate." He glanced back at Keira.

I thanked him and followed the direction Kalvin said that Greyson had gone. Buzzing insects and chirping birds were the only noises around me. The air was still. Voices echoed from the camp, gradually fading as I ventured further away.

A twig snapped.

The handle of my blade was in my palm. Turning around, I started to pull it out.

"Woah!" Greyson raised his hands in a mocking gesture, eyeing my blade coming out of its sheath. "Friend, not foe."

"You shouldn't sneak up on me like that." My voice was more upset than I meant for it to sound.

"And you shouldn't be so strict all the time." He frowned, dropping his hands. "You really need to loosen up."

"What do you mean?" I asked, looking away from the pain in his eyes.

"Something's stressing you out. Noah said it looked like you were having a nightmare last night." He reached out and grabbed my hand, pulling me close. "Come with me."

"Where are you going?"

"Do you trust me?"

I narrowed my eyes at Greyson but nodded.

"Then hold on."

Greyson shifted, his hands gripping my waist, and then his red wings caught air. My feet flew off the ground.

I wrapped my arms around his neck as we twisted and turned through the trees, the air thick with the promise of rain. We erupted through the canopy and finally slowed down. My feet found a large branch that was trying to stretch away from the tree and into the sky.

Once firmly on the branch, Greyson released me and moved to sit down next to me. His wings contracted, and he looked off into the distance. His shoulders were tight, and his back was hunched as he gripped the branch underneath us.

I stayed quiet. It confused me why he would have brought me up there. He wasn't saying anything, and the silence started to feel awkward.

His voice was gentle and low. "What are you so stressed about?" He didn't wait for me to answer. "Look, I get it, your father was wrong to treat you the way he did. But before all of this, at school, you seemed so lost in your thoughts, but you also didn't seem stressed or sad. Now, you seem so closed off and tense. You don't seem like yourself, Elisia." Greyson glanced at me for a second. "I'm sorry. I didn't know you at school and I really don't know you now. It just seems like something's wrong, and I don't want you to keep it all bottled up inside. That's all." He tightened his grip on his legs and turned his head farther away from me.

I didn't mean to change the subject, but I suddenly needed to know. "Why are you doing this? Why are you dropping your normal life to help a world you didn't even know existed two weeks ago?"

His head snapped back to me, his green eyes wide, and his mouth open. "Why am I..." His face softened while he processed my question. "Honestly, I'm not sure. I think, in the beginning, I was just swept up in the discovery of what I was and where I came from. You have no idea how it feels to not know your heritage. I knew I belonged in Perfidious, and when you decided to leave Coalfell, I just had this feeling that if I didn't follow you, I'd lose it all."

"But you don't have to put a target on your back to be in Perfidious. Being the king's heir puts your life in danger." My voice felt fragile but thankfully sounded strong.

"Someone once told me that being in this world would be risky for any half-breed. By doing this, by fighting the Council, I'd be helping make it a better world, one I could feel proud of being a part of. Plus, who knows if it will even come down to a fight. I can be quite charming." There was a gleam in his eyes as he slowly leaned toward me.

I laughed. "Oh yeah. So charming you had the whole cheerleading squad chasing after you."

He sighed dramatically. "Yup. But the one person I had an interest in never really showed much interest in me. I mean, Noah had to threaten me for me to even talk to her."

He glanced over at me.

I looked away from him. "Really? What happened there?"

He raised his eyebrows. "You've got all these questions, but you never answered mine."

"And what question was that?"

I turned to face him. His face was inches from mine. My breath caught, and my chest felt tight. I smelled his scent, somewhere in the middle of fried rice and toasted marshmallows, but in a good way.

"What's wrong?" His eyes were unmoving as he rested his hand on my shoulder.

I had to look away to speak.

I sighed. "I think it's a mix of dealing with Erlan and these dreams...it's all messing with my head."

Greyson's hand softly touched my chin and turned my head towards him. "It's all going to be okay. Things might seem difficult right now, but that's why we left. We're letting things cool down before returning."

"I guess," I whispered.

Greyson's eyes flickered to my lips, and he moved his hand to my cheek. If he moved any closer, his lips would collide with mine.

My heartbeat spiked as I quickly turned my entire body around. Heat rose to my cheeks and replaced the warmth from his hand. I looked back at him. I was sure my face looked more shocked than I felt.

"Um. I'm sorry. I shouldn't have...Did you not want to..." He wouldn't look me in the eyes. "Should we..."

"We should head back." I spoke quickly. "They're probably wondering where we are."

My voice didn't sound strong anymore, and my mind wasn't processing everything that just happened.

Thankfully, Greyson nodded and expanded his wings. He lifted us into the air, and it only took a matter of seconds for us to land in the middle of the camp. He gently set us down as everyone looked. I couldn't take how awkward everything felt, so I walked straight to the cabin I'd be sleeping in.

"Elisia!" Greyson pleaded from behind me.

I turned around and half-heartedly tried to look like everything was fine, but I didn't care if it really looked that way.

"We'll talk later, okay?" I turned and entered the cabin.

Alone at last, I started pacing. Greyson tried to kiss me. What the hell?

Greyson tried to kiss *me*.

He really had feelings for me. Did I have feelings for him?

I mean I liked him, but I didn't know if I liked him like that. I probably should have guessed from how overly sweet he'd been to me the last couple of weeks. He even invited me to the pool party. I should have questioned it then, but I was so used to having a flirty guy as my best friend that I didn't think anything of his actions.

My hand absentmindedly raised to my lips, and my fingers traced their curves. They felt foreign.

Could I have feelings for him?

He was hot and caring, but what did I really know about him...

Wait. Scratch that.

I know more about him than anyone at school now. My hand fisted in my hair as I sat down on the bed and pulled my knees up to rest my forehead on. I was never good at that kind of stuff. I'd never had guys going after me. It was hard for me to believe that anyone could see me as more than a friend.

I almost didn't realize that someone had come into the cabin. The person didn't say a single word as he plopped down next to me. His rough hand rubbed circles on my shoulder blade.

I knew exactly who it was.

"Why'd you come in here?" I asked Kalvin, my voice muffled by my arms.

His hand gripped my shoulder and pulled me closer until I was leaning against him. He continued to rub my shoulder comfortingly. "Ya didn't seem okay. Did somethin' happen?"

"Yeah," I said, not that I wanted to admit it. "I'm just confused and needed some time alone."

"Did I not give ya enough time?" He pulled away

slightly and looked down at me. "I tried to make sure ya had some time, but I thought if something happened, and I left ya alone with your thoughts for too long, ya'd go crazy."

I chuckled and pushed myself up, sitting with my feet over the edge. I took a deep breath before my voice lost all of its humor.

"Greyson tried to kiss me."

There was silence for a long time, and it made me nervous. I looked at Kalvin. He had the same expression that he had that morning, but I still couldn't tell what he was thinking. His body tightened.

"Do I need to kill him?"

I rolled my eyes. "No. I...I saw him lean in to kiss me, and I freaked out. I never thought he'd like me. Why me? There are a ton of girls that like him at school. He's popular and could have any girl he wanted."

"And how do ya feel about him?"

I rested my head back against his chest. Being so close to him brought me comfort.

"I don't know. I feel like I have too much going on to worry about someone having feelings for me. I feel stupid, and I feel like I should have seen it coming, but I didn't."

Kalvin's chest vibrated.

I leaned back. "Why are you laughing?"

He coughed to hide his laughter. "Elisia, ya haven't noticed at all? It's not like Greyson tried to keep it a secret. He made it very obvious." He said the last part through his teeth.

I lifted my hands in defeat. "It's not like I have all these guys flirting with me or confessing their feelings for me. The only person I've ever known to flirt with me is you. But I'm pretty sure flirting with girls is, like, your hobby."

Kalvin's shoulders fell slightly. "What makes you think that? Maybe all I see is you." There was no humor in his voice.

I giggled at his comment. There was no way he was serious. How many girls had he said *that* line to? But somehow his flirty attitude relaxed me.

"Oh please." I nudged him. "I've seen you in the market. All the girls flock around you."

He hesitantly opened his mouth to say something, but then closed it and looked away from me. "Here is my sage advice. If things are too complicated for ya right now to worry about him in that way, just tell him ya can't deal with his feelings and he needs to leave ya alone." Kalvin looked back at me and shook his head. "I mean, to let ya deal with it in your own time. Otherwise, tell him you're not interested."

"Okay, but do me a favor? Keep him distracted so I don't have to deal with it tonight. I just need time to myself right now."

Kalvin nodded, the corners of his lips curling up. "Yup. I don't mind keepin' him away from ya."

27

Kalvin fulfilled his promise and kept Greyson busy for the rest of the night. I didn't mean to avoid him, but it made it easier to think about how I felt. Whenever Kalvin saw me thinking too hard, he'd wink at me. It made me roll my eyes and smile every time.

After dinner, everyone dispersed. I didn't pay attention to where they went. I just stared into the fire. watching it shift and crackle. It was comforting. I almost didn't want to put it out, but we didn't want to risk starting a forest fire by leaving it burning.

I grabbed the pail of water next to me. The light from the fire darkened unnaturally before I could splash it with water. I set the bucket back down. Keira appeared at the other side of the fire. I had never met a shadow before, and I wasn't sure what to expect from her.

Her dark features—black hair, dark chocolate brown eyes, and mocha skin—made her seem like she indeed covered by shadows. Long silhouettes around me were moving like waves in water. She controlled them, manipulated them.

"So, I've gathered this much since you've arrived." Keira started to walk around the fire. "The two half-breeds are annoying...You're a mess that doesn't know what she wants...The human isn't as stupid as I thought, which was surprising...Then, there is the fact that Greyson is part fairy. He healed a cut the human got earlier, but I also know Greyson can shapeshift. Oh, and let's not forget the human part of him—the Anchor proves that. That means you all ran away, from wherever you came from, because he's the freakin' king's heir." Keira arched her eyebrow. "How'd I do?"

I blinked a couple of times. She'd found out more about us in one day than I was able to figure out about her. I crossed my arms as though it didn't bother me.

"Not bad. You're observant. But what are you going to do with this information now?"

I assessed her. She wasn't giving off a vindictive vibe. Keira was definitely smart, but I couldn't figure out if she was trustworthy yet.

"Let me help." She loosened her stance as she held my gaze, and I felt the thickness in the night air thin around me. "Look, I'm not gonna turn you all over to the Council, or some shit like that. I'm a half-breed, too." She turned around and dropped the corner of her long sleeve to show the Anchor on her shoulder. It looked like a question mark without the dot, with another upside-down question mark meeting it in a broken spiral. "If you know anything about Shadows, there haven't been many purebloods in a long time. My species could be helpful if it comes to a war."

"We are trying to avoid a war. If no war comes, how

would you help?" I asked, trying to get as much out of her as possible.

Keira laughed. "Simple. I'm sneaky—not many people notice me if I don't want them to. I can help keep an eye on things. Make sure no one's hiding in my shadows. Plus, I have more abilities than you or Kalvin. I can help train them. I can tell they pick up on things easily, but they aren't exactly flawless, and their mistakes are obvious."

I uncrossed my arms, taking a step towards her. "It's not exactly my decision."

Keira smirked.

My eyes narrowed. "But you knew that. So why did you approach *me*? Couldn't you have told all of this to Greyson?"

Keira shrugged. "I could've, but I wanted to talk to you about it. You seem much more like a leader than a follower. Plus, I wanna challenge you to a fight. No prize for the winner, but then you could see what I'm made of and how beneficial it would be for me to join you." She shifted her weight and looked behind her at the boys who were coming out of the cabin. "I wanna see what a little half-elf is made of."

Keira's demeanor was strong and confident. I couldn't tell if she was faking her playfulness or if she was sincerely wanting to help.

A fight might be a good way to find out.

"Okay." I nodded, and excitement sparked through me at the thought of sparring with someone new. "Just tell me when."

Keira shifted her weight as the shadows started to feel thick again. "Now."

Before I could process what she said, Keira threw three knives directly at me.

I dropped to the ground as they flew over me and disappeared into the shadows. I stood, my Tonfas in my hands, and easily blocked the next set of blades before making my advance.

Keira was ready for a head on attack. I dropped my body, slide-tackling her, and turned my blades back to block her knives. The sound of metal hitting metal twanged in the air. I took a couple steps back, watching her.

She recovered fast, extending her pointer finger at me and signaling for me to come at her again. It was like she watched every single move I made with a clarity I couldn't understand. I looked her in the eyes and realized she wasn't looking directly at me. Keira was watching behind me.

Following her sightline, I saw my silhouette stretched out on the ground. I pushed her back, then reached out to kick her, continuing the kicks until she was closer to the fire. The light elongated my shadow over the camp so she could no longer make out my movements.

Keira frowned, her body starting to disappear into the darkness at her feet. A black mist swirled around my own. I tried to follow it, but there were too many shadows.

Suddenly, I felt two blades poke my back. I froze and looked over my shoulder at Keira's amused expression.

"Damn," she stated, blades still poking my back. "You're faster than I thought, and you picked up on the fact that I was reading your movements through your shadow, didn't you? Shit, I really didn't think you would." Keira removed the knives and slightly bowed to me. "The boys are standing ready to attack me, so I'm pretty sure that means you win. There is no way I'd be able to take on all four of you." Her smile faltered slightly. "Must feel damn good to have them watch your back."

My eyes left Keira to look at Kalvin, Greyson, and Noah. Their weapons out and ready to attack.

I laughed. "Yeah. I've never fought someone with your abilities. I have to say you're pretty good, but we both landed a couple of blows."

I looked down at the cut on her forearm. Her dark clothes covered up a good amount of skin, but she was holding her side, I imagine that one of my kicks had left a bruise.

"Elisia," Greyson said. "What's going on?"

I explained what had happened to everyone. Kalvin and Noah agreed that Keira would be very helpful in training. Greyson kept quiet while monitoring me. I watched him out of the corner of my eye.

I really needed to talk to him.

After the excitement faded, everyone started to return to their cabins for the night. I stayed back by the fire with Greyson.

"Heal this for me?" I asked him, showing him a small cut on my shoulder. "It was from her surprising me with the first three knives."

Greyson nodded. He came over and slowly moved my sleeve up my arm so that he could put his hand fully on the cut. "It's not deep." The green light flickered, and he moved his hand away. "Look, Elisia, I'm sorry. I— I really shouldn't have...shouldn't have tried to kiss you like that. I thought—"

I put my hand up to his mouth to keep him from

continuing. "No, *I'm* sorry. I shouldn't have reacted the way
I did."

Greyson arched his eyebrow. "So, does that mean I still
have a shot?"

"I don't know what I feel for you, and I can't do this
right now." My pulse was racing, and I knew if I didn't get
it out, I wouldn't have the courage later. "There is so much
going on with you being the king's heir, my ongoing fight
with Erlan, and everything. I'm too overwhelmed to figure
out what my feelings for you mean."

My palms were sweating. I looked away from his eyes.
I'd never had to deal with that kind of thing. People at
school usually kept to their own groups, and it wasn't like I
could get close to anyone at school, especially guys. The
only male I'd ever been close to was Kalvin.

Greyson took a deep breath. "Well, I guess that's fair. I
can give you some time. There is no rush, okay?" He
reached out, moved my hair out of my eyes, and chuckled.
"You're cute when you're flustered."

I hit him. My cheeks were getting hot, and I knew I was
probably blushing. Greyson laughed at me. I stomped
away from him. He chased after me, making apologies and
more jokes.

I needed to just have friends. I could think about the
rest later.

28

The next day, we began training. Kalvin wanted to make a schedule so that we'd be training on different techniques with different people.

I was to train them in hand-to-hand combat. Greyson was definitely getting better, and I didn't have to go easy on him anymore. Noah was trying, but without monster blood, he could only get so far. He'd need to get stronger if he wanted a chance to compete.

I was sparring with Noah, attempting to get him to learn how to read my movements. He grunted and kicked me square in the shin. It reminded me of an upset kid pouting. I avoided all of his attacks and stopped to pull him aside. His body was tense, and his lips were thin.

"Noah, how far have you gotten in the books I gave you?" I asked him, trying to sound polite.

"I've read two of them but still haven't gotten through the other two. I want to focus on fighting and getting stronger," Noah said with a forced monotone.

"Okay, but I also think that you need to focus on your

studies. We can always find you some more books, or we can teach you if you have questions the books don't answer. Knowing the enemy is equally as important as the actual battle and fighting," I explained.

Noah waved his hand at me and turned away. "Whatever, I'm gonna see if Kalvin can teach me some other weapons. Later."

He left, and I ended up just sending Greyson to work with Kalvin for weapon training. I decided to work with my Tonfas for a while. I was getting comfortable with them, but I still needed more practice.

Eventually, Keira stepped in to train the boys. I stopped to watch. She started with hand-to-hand and then allowed them to pick up weapons. Keira danced circles around them as she dodged their attacks, jumping in and out of shadows. She would throw a dagger here and there, but she never really aimed directly at them. I didn't know much about her, but so far, I didn't get a bad feeling about her. Keira seemed sincere, but I wasn't sure how much I believed it.

Suddenly, arms wrapped around me, and I was thrown over a shoulder. I knew it was Kalvin from his laugh as he ran around the fire pit. I giggled hysterically and forgot about Keira.

"Kalvin!" I said, pushing down on his shoulder. "Put me down."

"Nah. You're my princess, and I'm the great dragon that gets to sweep ya off your feet." He finally stopped running and looked over his shoulder at me, grinning.

"Yeah, I don't think that's how the story goes," I said, not even trying to get out of his grip anymore. "Isn't the dragon supposed to hide the princess away until the prince comes to save her?"

He shrugged his shoulders and started jogging towards the food cabin. "Maybe, but what if the dragon is hiding her away because he loves her? What would the princess do then?"

"I'm not sure. You really have a bony shoulder." I chuckled, adjusting where his shoulder was pressed into my abdomen.

Kalvin finally set me down once we were inside the food cabin. "Help me get dinner ready?"

"Sure," I said, scanning the canned goods and pastas on the shelves. We still didn't have much to work with since Keira ate most of it before we got there. "Meatless spaghetti? We have noodles, sauce, mushrooms, and spinach in cans. That could be good, right? Unless one of us wants to go hunting for some meat?" I questioned.

Kalvin nodded. "That'll be fine." He started grabbing the ingredients from the shelf and was quiet for several minutes.

"But seriously," Kalvin said, seemingly deep in thought. "If the princess was with the dragon all that time, why would she want to leave him for some prince who just shows up and says he likes her? She doesn't even know him, and the dragon has been protecting her all that time."

I shook my head slightly. "What are you talking about?"

Kalvin quickly turned his face to a smirk. "Nothing. I'm just mumbling about nonsense."

I forced a smile. There was more to what Kalvin said, but I wasn't sure if he was just being goofy or serious. I let it go. I'd known Kalvin a long time. If he had something he wanted to talk about, he'd talk about it when he was ready. I'd probably bring it up later, but right then, I focused on dinner.

While we ate, Greyson healed Noah's small cuts and talked about how excited he was about his progress. He held most of the conversation. I zoned out, more focused on other things. Greyson was grinning like everything was okay, but at the same time, he kept fidgeting. He seemed uncomfortable. Something was definitely wrong.

After I was finished eating, I started to grab dishes to take them down to the river.

Keira beat me to it. "Don't worry about this shit. You basically made dinner. We can clean up. Dragon boy, help me."

"What? I helped with dinner, too," Kalvin said, throwing his hands in the air.

"You're gonna make me go all by myself? What if I need a strong dragon to protect me?" She stuck out her lip and gave Kalvin the puppy eyes.

I rolled my eyes and tried to ignore Keira. She seemed to be clinging to Kalvin a little too much, and I wasn't sure I liked it.

Kalvin sighed, then grabbed some dishes and followed her. Greyson and Noah were taking care of the garbage, leaving me taskless.

"Since you guys have this all under control, I'm gonna get some firewood. I could use the walk anyway." I turned to leave.

A gentle hand on my shoulder stopped me.

"Elisia, is something wrong? You seem like you're worried about something," Greyson asked.

"Shouldn't I be asking you that? You're the one that's

trying too hard to make everyone smile," I said, and his hand dropped immediately.

"I'm just trying not to think too much about what could happen. I know Noah's mom is probably freaking out by now that she hasn't been able to get a hold of us, and it makes me worry that she may have figured out we lied."

I nodded. "I'll be back in a little bit, and we can talk about it then, okay?" I tried to go out for firewood again but saw Keira and Kalvin at the gate. She was carrying the clean dishes, and he was carrying an arm full of firewood. I turned back to Greyson. "On second thought, do you want to talk in the cabin for a bit?"

Greyson looked over my shoulder at Kalvin. He smirked mischievously at him, looked back at me, and pulled me close. "I have a better idea."

His wings popped out and, suddenly, we were in the air.

I clung to him as I watched the camp disappear in the distance.

"Greyson, where are we going?" I yelled, but it was obvious he either couldn't hear me or chose not to answer.

It wasn't long before he slowed down for us to sit in a tree. He put me down first, landed, and put his wings away. I was about to explain to him that he can't just pick me up and start flying, but his glazed over eyes stopped me. His lips were pressed together, and his attention was directed ahead of him. The sun had already gone down, but it was clear he wasn't looking at the sky.

"Do you think we should go back?" Greyson asked. I waited a moment for him to continue, but he didn't.

"Why would we? We just got here." I prompted.

"Well, why did we even come out here? I know you had your problems with your dad, but I don't feel like that's a good enough reason to just leave anymore. We just disappeared." He brought his knees up to his chest and wrapped his arms around them as he leaned against the trunk of the tree.

I placed my hand on his shoulder. "Where did this come from? Literally yesterday you were saying how you didn't have a problem coming with us."

"I was reading the history book my mom left me. The way it talked about King Lawrence, my grandfather. It explained how he knew exactly what to do, how he never ran away, even after the attempts on his life. He was described as a strong king and a problem-solver. Not once did they say that he ignored a problem. He fought only when he needed to, and everything else he solved by compromise. Apparently, the only reason he got overthrown was because he didn't care what kind of monster someone was and ended up marrying a fairy. He had views about monsters and half-breeds that a lot of monsters didn't agree with." He paused and looked at me. "I don't want to be viewed as a cowardly heir. I don't want to tarnish his legacy like that."

"Who said you were running away?"

"Keira told me how running away sometimes is the best answer, but she's wrong. I wasn't trying to run away, and I don't want others to think that's what I did."

I bit my lip. "So, you want to go back?"

"No, I want all of us to go back. Like I said, I have this feeling that I can't do this without you. We'll all be there, and we'll be able to keep you safe from your father. I want

—no—I *need* to be front and center if I decide to overthrow the Council."

There was a long moment of silence. I shifted on the branch, but my brain couldn't process words.

Greyson's excitement drained the longer I took to respond to him.

"Are you sure that you want to become king? If you start telling others, you can't back down. You're talking about war and going for it one hundred percent. Are you sure?"

"I'm not sure." He started talking faster as though he had thought about it more than once. "Either way, I can't have Noah's mom track us down because we lied to her about where we were going. We haven't talked to her since. And I don't want to fear your father coming after us and dragging you away from me—I mean, *us*. If I want to become king, I need more half-breeds on our side. I can't gain support by hiding. And then there's my training..."

I started laughing. "Okay, okay. I get your point. You've thought about this a lot. But you're probably right. We should head back home." My stomach tightened at the thought of having to face my father again, but we didn't have a lot of food or money left, meaning we had to think of something. "Let's head back to the camp, and we'll discuss it with everyone in the morning."

Greyson nodded and extended his wings, flying faster than before. We landed back in the camp in no time. Greyson went straight to the cabin to talk to Noah, and I went to the food shelter to grab some water. I found what I needed and went to exit.

Voices traveled from the gate into the camp. Kalvin and

Keira exited the woods together. I froze. He was carrying firewood, and she was just walking with him.

"Tell me something." Kalvin told her. "Why do you insist on following me?"

"The hell are you talking about?" Keira questioned back.

She looked in my direction, and I hid behind the door. I wasn't sure why I was hiding. It was just a reaction.

I heard Keira continue. "I thought it'd be safer to not have people go off on their own."

"Of course, ya did. But I doubt that's the whole truth," he challenged. Wood pieces clunked against one another as he set the small logs down.

"Well, it seems like that's what Greyson and Elisia do. You know, they disappear together a lot."

"Yup. I know," he said through his teeth.

My breath caught. *Why would he be annoyed?*

I peeked around the door and saw Keira cross her arms. "Do you know you make it hella obvious?"

"What do you..." Kalvin started, but Keira made an exaggerated breath and he stopped talking.

"You know exactly what I mean. Damn. You're basically in love with Elisia, and you choose not to tell her for some stupid reason. On top of that, you mope around after you found out some other guy's beat you to it. Get a grip you stupid dragon."

My body immediately seized. My mind froze. Surely, she meant platonically right?

Kalvin panicked and looked around him. "Will you shut up? You don't know what you're talking about. I have my reasons for not telling her. Plus, you're one to talk. The only reason you're helping us out and trying to gain Elisia's trust is because you have nowhere else to go. I know you're on the run from something. I'm not sure why yet, but you're not the only one that's good at reading people. I didn't trust you from the moment we got here, and so far, that hasn't changed."

Kalvin's muscles were tight as he stood over Keira. He was at least a foot taller than her.

Keira's mouth fell open. She didn't say another word as she walked away, disappearing into a cabin. He took a deep breath and walked the opposite way. Directly towards me.

I couldn't even move. I was standing in the doorway, and as soon as he looked up, he would see me. But my body wasn't listening to my brain. I should move. Come up with an excuse. Say I heard nothing. But I heard it all, and I didn't know what it meant.

Kalvin walked with his head down. My feet came into view. His eyes snapped up and met mine. His pupils went from slits to normal circles, his mouth slightly ajar.

"Elisia, I..." He stopped. It was as if his brain froze.

"Water," I said stupidly, holding up the water bottle. "I was getting water. D-Do you want some?" I asked, trying to act normal.

"Uh, that, um, sounds good." He kept wiping his hands on his sides as he watched me get another bottle of water.

We were silent as we drank.

"You heard." Kalvin didn't need to ask. He knew.

His upset tone made my chest ache. Kalvin wasn't explaining himself or denying it. Did that mean it was true? Why wouldn't he tell me? Maybe he was waiting for a good time? I did just tell him that I couldn't deal with Greyson's feelings, and I never really gave him a chance.

He knew I didn't take his flirting seriously. I made up my mind. I was just going to pretend I didn't hear that part.

"Yeah," I said. "Keira's running away from something? What do you think it is?" I took another sip of my water.

His eyes narrowed, and he blinked a couple times. "Oh. Um, I'm not sure."

"I guess it makes sense why you've been watching her now. I thought you thought she was cute or something." I cracked a smile, hoping to just ignore the other stuff. I guess Kalvin caught my drift.

The corners of his lips raised a little. "No, she's definitely not my type."

"Well, monitor her for me okay? I don't fully trust her either," I said, as he drank more of his water. "I'm gonna head to bed. Goodnight, Kalvin."

He pulled me into a hug, surprising me. His arms were strong, but gentle around me. I hugged him back.

Then, Kalvin whispered, just barely audible, "Thank you."

29

"**E**lisia?" I moved farther under my covers and groaned, but the annoying person pulled the covers away and shook me. "Elisia!"

"What?" I opened my eyes to see Keira and darkness around us. "Keira, it's the middle of the night. What do you want?"

Her eyes were wide, and she kept looking behind her. "Something's wrong."

I sat up. "Why should I believe you?"

She placed her hand on the shadow of my bed. "The shadows are quiet."

I raised my eyebrow at her. She continued.

"Meaning, nothing is moving. Nothing is making noise. No creatures. No animals. Nothing."

Before she could say anything else, I got out of the bed and walked past her out of the cabin.

Then I listened. I listened for any sign of any kind of life. But there was nothing. No movement at all.

She was right.

Something was very wrong.

I turned back towards her. "Keira, go wake the boys. I'm gonna look around the perimeter."

I grabbed my Tonfas and ran out to the gate. There was nothing outside. An eerie quiet settled around me as I jogged around the camp. I climbed a tree and looked around the area. I almost thought I was imagining it, but a couple trees moved in the distance.

Something big was coming straight for us.

I jumped down and ran back to the camp. The others were standing around outside the cabins, checking weapons and talking.

They looked at me.

I increased my pace. "We need to leave now. Something's coming."

"What's coming?" Kalvin asked, pulling his daggers out.

"I'm not sure. There are no animals around at all. Not even mosquitos. Whatever it is, even insects know to stay away from it. It's big enough to move trees in the distance, and it's coming fast."

I started walking back to the camp gate. A monstrous howl stopped me in my tracks, and I instinctively backed up.

"I've never heard anything like that." Noah's voice shook.

The creature became visible. It didn't look like any beast I had ever seen. Horns that looked like tree limbs but were sharp as knives sprouted from his bull-shaped head. His body was still shifting. I wasn't sure what he was turning into. He growled and peered down at us, seeming to grow several feet taller with each step he took inside the gate.

"I've finally found you," the creature spoke.

I heard Greyson behind me whisper, "It's the shapeshifter."

I unsheathed my blades.

The shapeshifter launched at us.

I dodged to the side and looked back to make sure everyone got out of its way. Greyson was in the air with Noah. Kalvin and Keira ran behind one of the cabins. But the shapeshifter was only after one person. Greyson tried to fly higher as the beast lunged for him again. The creature's backbones extended.

He was growing wings.

I took my Tonfas and jumped onto its back. My blades dug deep into one of his half-formed wings. Gravity pulled me down, causing my Tofonas to rip long lines down the beasts back. He howled in pain and tried to buck me off. I jumped off and Kalvin jumped in. He sliced the other half-formed wing with his two daggers.

We had the beast surrounded, and I thought we could finish the fight, but he started to shrink. His body got smaller, and his tail grew longer. The shapeshifter had scales like the first time we saw him, about the size of a crocodile, but with the claws of a banshee. He lunged at me, twice as fast as before. His tail swung at Kalvin, knocking him to the side.

I jumped back.

The shapeshifter kept coming at me.

My blades cut into his arms with every punch. His claws shifted again and lengthened like giant eagle talons. He grabbed onto my upper body, nails ripping into my shoulders. I tried to muffle my yelp. I needed to focus on fighting instead of my injuries.

"Elisia!"

Greyson began his descent, coming down to attack.

"No! Stay out of reach!" I moved back as the shapeshifter tried to dig his other claw into me. "You're who he's after. As long as we keep him on the ground, he can't get to you."

Something moved past my feet. Dark mist snaked around the shapeshifter's ankles, holding him in place. Smirking, I stabbed my tonfa into his wrist. He shrieked, releasing his hold on me. I backed up. He tried to follow me, but the shadows held him in place.

Anger flashed in his eyes. He turned towards Keira, his gaze locking on her hands. They looked like they were holding onto something.

He knew she was a shadow.

I put my hand over the wound on my shoulder and scanned the sky. Greyson looked down. His eyes locked on me.

Noah struggled in his arms. "We need to help them!"

Greyson broke eye contact with me to get a better grip on Noah. "Stop moving, or I'll drop you."

"Then drop me!" Noah yelled in frustration as he tried to get Greyson to let go of him.

Kalvin and Keira stepped away from the shapeshifter. His limbs grew bigger and morphed from scales to fur. I ran at him, trying to distract him from changing. I raised my Tonfa, extending the point outward.

A snake-like tail darted out.

It struck me in the stomach, forcing the air from my lungs. I couldn't catch my breath as I flew through the air.

My body broke through the top of one of the cabins. I landed on something soft, and my body seized.

I looked around my body to assess my injuries. It seemed like I only had shallow cuts and bruises. That could have been a lot worse.

I tried to get up, but pain shocked my senses. My hip was bleeding. It wasn't a shallow cut either. I took a deep breath. I couldn't quit. He'd kill us all if we didn't get the fight to swing in our favor.

I ripped a piece of the sheet next to me and tied it around my hip like a makeshift bandage. I forced myself up and limped out of the wreckage.

A full-sized griffin stood in front of me. I checked the wings. It looked like he wouldn't be able to fly, but that didn't mean much. He was on two lion legs, swatting at Greyson and Noah with giant paws.

Kalvin sat next to the destroyed shed. He had a cut on his forehead, and his shirt was torn up a bit, but his main focus was on his ankle.

"Are you okay?" I asked.

I helped him stand. He tried to put weight on his ankle and hissed. "Yup, but I'm probably out of commission. What do we do with a creature that doesn't stop shifting?"

I looked around us for Keira. I spied her trying to use shadows to keep the griffin-shapeshifter away from Greyson. "I'm not sure. We could try baiting it, then attacking it from above? Like we did to the snake?"

"I'll see if Keira can help me get to the woods. We'll get into position. Think you can get 'em to follow you and Greyson?"

"Yeah. He has tunnel vision right now." I started to walk away from him, then yelled back, "Just hurry!"

I used my speed to run past the snake tail that was still swinging around, slicing a cut into the shifter's back legs. He turned towards me on all fours, easily twelve feet tall. I ran and had to expect the others were doing their parts.

He was on my heels as I ran through the only cabin left standing, jumping through the tiny window on the far side. I tiptoed through the darkest area next to the gate. Keeping to the shadow, I looked back. The griffin was distracted with destroying the cabin, thinking I was still inside.

I saw Greyson healing Kalvin's ankle.

"Everyone good?" I whispered.

Kalvin gave me a thumbs up. Keira nodded and grabbed Noah. She didn't seem to have sustained too many injuries, but she was also fighting from a distance.

"I'm taking Noah by shadow. Kalvin will follow us on foot. Go straight out of the gate and head to the river. We'll be able to adjust when we see him," she whispered, sinking into the shadows with Noah.

He stared in disbelief as his body disappeared.

Kalvin took off out the gate. I looked back to see Greyson looking over me. "You're hurt."

His eyes suddenly widened.

In one swift motion, he reached out to me and pulled me to him, bringing his wings down hard. We were in the air before I even realized what had happened.

Below us, the griffin's paws crashed down on where we had been standing. Greyson flew closer to the ground and started for the gate. The shapeshifter ran right behind us, just barely out of reach.

I put my hand around my mouth and Greyson's ear. "Lower. We don't want him looking up."

I scanned the trees and saw the others up ahead. The shapeshifter followed close behind and had no time to respond. Keira and Kalvin came crashing down onto its back. Before he could shift into something else, Kalvin took a sword and plunged it into the back of the beast's head. Greyson quickly turned around and landed right in front of it. My Tonfas were out and ready as we approached.

The life drained from the shapeshifter's eyes.

30

I stumbled backwards and stopped, a tree at my back. My injuries ached and burned as I used the tree for support. I kept an eye on the creature in front of me, not believing he was really dead. His yellow eyes were lifeless. My breaths slowly evened out, and I hissed in pain as the adrenaline started to leave my body.

A rustle came from behind us.

I quickly moved to put myself in between my friends and the noise. I unsheathed my Tonfas and felt my body pulse. My knees felt weak, as though they wouldn't hold me up, but I had to ignore it. I waited as the bush shook, and a dark figure emerged.

I noticed it was Noah before I attacked.

"No danger from me." He stomped past me and started toward the camp.

Slowly, everyone followed him. I tried to stand, but my pain levels spiked. My weight fell back against the tree. Without a word, Kalvin was at my side. He put his arm underneath mine and helped me walk forward. I gave him a small smile, but he didn't look me in the eyes. His attention was on my bleeding shoulder.

Back at the camp, I slowly laid down on a piece of ground without debris. I closed my eyes to assess my injuries. Both of my shoulders had bad gashes. There was pain coming from my left hip. Multiple bruises everywhere and cuts on my arms from my Tonfas.

Wonderful.

I opened my eyes, feeling a moment of deja vu. I searched my memories for a time that I had been hurt in the same capacity, but nothing came to the surface. I shrugged it off as I sat up. I couldn't suppress the groan that rose to my lips. A sharp stinging radiated through my body.

Suddenly, a pair of hands were helping me lay back down. I looked to my side to see Kalvin.

"You should stay laying down. You took a lot of damage," Kalvin said as he looked me over. "Greyson is healing Keira right now, and then he'll be over here to work on healing you."

I sat up against Kalvin's wishes. "I'm fine to sit. Why is he healing her, anyway? I didn't see her get thrown around like we did."

Kalvin rolled his eyes. "She had a couple cuts and bitched about it until Greyson agreed."

My eyes searched for him as Kalvin spoke. Greyson's eyes met mine for a split second before he looked back to Keira.

My heart ached.

Kalvin was still talking. "She probably has a low pain tolerance. It's not like she really does a whole lot of contact fightin'. She fights with her throwin' knives and her shadows from a distance."

I rolled my eyes. "Do me a favor. Don't let him heal me all the way until he gets a little rest. Just enough to stop the bleeding. He already healed your ankle, and that was most likely broken. He can't deal with too much more." Kalvin opened his mouth to object, but I placed my hand on his, and he closed his mouth. "Please?"

Kalvin's shoulders slumped in defeat. "Fine, but while he rests, you're staying put. If ya try to move, I'm knockin' ya out."

I saw movement in my peripheral. Greyson jogged over to us. He tried to heal every injury I had, but Kalvin and I made sure he didn't.

After he healed my shoulders enough to stop the bleeding, I saw the sweat on his brow and the shaking of his hands. But once he closed the gash on my hip, he staggered as he moved. Green light illuminated but flickered. He wasn't strong enough to keep going.

I grabbed his hands and pushed them away.

"No more," I stated, but he looked like he wanted to resist. "You need rest and aren't going to do us any good if you die on us. Take a break. I won't bleed out while you recover your strength."

He nodded as he plopped down next to me. Greyson fell asleep quickly, and Kalvin grabbed some food for us to snack on.

Hours passed. I'm not sure how many.

I looked over the trees at some light shining through, realizing it was morning already. Greyson started to wake and looked around groggily.

"Elisia?"

I looked around at my friends to see who said my name, but I didn't recognize the voice as any of theirs.

"Elisia!" I looked around again and saw a misplaced silhouette on the ground.

As I gazed upward for its source, I spied Lexon floating down.

"Oh, little Elisia! I'm so glad I found you." He touched down, shed his rock exterior, and kneeled next to me, assessing my injuries, his stone wings covering the sun from my eyes. "Are you okay? I came as soon as I could."

"Who are you?" Keira asked.

I looked over at her and waved for her to stand down. She slid her knives back into her gear but left her hands in easy reach of them.

"Everyone, this is Lexon. I've met him a few times in the old church ruins. He's the one I went to see on that day I kinda disappeared." I turned back to Lexon. "We're alright. Why did you come looking for me?"

"After I didn't hear from you about the king's heir, I got worried. I wanted to make sure nothing had happened to you on your journey to see the shapeshifter. I went to Coalfell to ask around for you, but I heard that you four had left." He stood up as Kalvin approached him. "It seemed as though you all literally disappeared. I didn't even know you were safe until I met a whisper, who told me a generalized idea of where you were. I figured you had your reasons and went to the castle to see if I could learn any new information. I overheard the shapeshifter reporting to the Council about your encounter. They granted him permission to 'take care of the problem.' I tried my hardest to find you after that, but this place isn't easy to find."

"That was kind of the point." I chuckled, but the little movement hurt. "So how did you find us?"

Lexon nodded, as though he was getting to that part. "I stopped at a village nearby, asking if they'd seen anything strange lately. They said they had seen a boy flying around east of there a couple times, but they didn't know of any winged creatures that lived in the area. I assumed that it was Greyson. I'm also guessing that's how the shapeshifter found you."

"Well, you just missed the fight," Greyson said, limping over. He extended his hand to Lexon. "You know so much about me; I feel I should introduce myself properly."

Lexon shook his hand and turned to me. "I already like this boy. But is everyone alright? Where is the shapeshifter?"

"Dead." Keira said, still standing apart from the group.

Lexon looked her over. "You, I do not recognize. What's your name, dear?"

"That's Keira. She's a newer addition to our group," I told him.

Lexon smiled at her, knowingly. "Hmm. Interesting." Then, he turned so he could face Greyson and myself. "But what prompted you to come all the way out here? As far as I know, the shapeshifter wasn't after you until after you'd left."

Kalvin answered before anyone else. "It's a long story, but this seemed the best place to hide from those who oppose the king's heir."

I knew he was talking about Erlan, but I was glad he wasn't blunt about that fact.

Lexon's eyes widened slightly. "Best place to *hide*?" He stood up and turned to Greyson. "My young king, you should be showing yourself to the world, gathering support and expressing that you only mean to help. Remain hidden, and rumors will spread. You want to be upfront about the change you wish to create. Show others you mean to restore the peace your grandfather created."

Greyson nodded. "I completely agree. I already talked to Noah and Elisia about it, and I was gonna talk to the rest of the group this morning, but then we were attacked."

"Well, if you wish, I could help you make a speedy return?" Lexon offered.

Noah looked at him questioningly. "How—and why—would you do that?"

Lexon turned to him, looking more human than I had ever seen him. "Well, there are three of us here that can travel long distances quickly. We could each carry a person. As for why, I was loyal to the old king, King Lawrence. That loyalty extends to his grandson, not those current monsters residing on the throne."

Greyson grinned proudly. "Well, I appreciate your loyalty. We might have to wait until later in the day to travel though. I am still weak from healing everyone, and I haven't fully healed Elisia yet."

Lexon nodded. "Okay. Then, we leave at sundown. That will provide your shadow with the best amount of darkness, but for us with wings, still enough light to see."

Greyson healed my remaining injuries the best he could, but he needed more rest. He slept nearly the entire day. We decided to leave our bags at the camp to limit the weight everyone would have to carry. Kalvin immediately took charge, telling everyone who to go with.

Lexon picked me up with one arm as we shot into the air. Greyson followed closely behind with Noah. I looked back to see Keira and Kalvin dissipate into the shadows, just a black mist below us jumping between silhouettes. The whole trip would probably take about three hours flying at top speed.

Knots twisted around in my stomach as I debated what to do when I got home.

31

Once we were just outside Coalfell, I told Lexon to set me down on the outskirts of the village. He frowned but complied with my request. I waved at Greyson to continue.

Lexon set me down. "May I ask why, little Elisia?"

I whispered to him so no one else would hear. "Don't take this the wrong way, but I don't want anyone to see you. You still have your position at the castle, which may come in handy someday. No one in the village can see that we know each other or that you helped us. Make sense?"

He nodded slowly. "I trust your judgement." And with that, he turned around to take off.

"Wait, Lexon." I called, and he turned back to face me. "Do you by chance know of a way to lie to an elf who can detect lies?"

"Hmm," he gave me a puzzled look but didn't question me. "I have heard rumors that a person can lie without detection when they have an herb called yarrow directly in between them and the elf."

My eyes widened. There was a chance my plan would work. "What does yarrow look like?"

Lexon scanned the ground and grabbed a small bunch of tiny white flowers. He handed it to me. "It looks like this. It's found almost everywhere, but if you plan to use this, I have to warn you. I have only heard of common yarrows working. I would ask your whisper friend if you have questions. He'd probably know more."

I nodded. "Thank you, Lexon."

I ran off to join my group, who I found already outside the Elders tent. Greyson summoned the Elders under the pretense of an emergency. We paced as we waited. They took their time, but they finally beckoned us into the tent.

As I walked in, I saw the annoyed faces of the Elders.

Drithro spoke first. "Elisia, we were in the middle of dinner."

Greyson stood in front of me to speak. "I'm sorry to have interrupted you, but we have an urgent request."

Yima answered. "We are eager to hear, King's Heir."

Greyson cleared his throat and seemed to hesitate. Yima nodded encouragingly to him.

Greyson took a deep breath and spoke clearly. "The Council knows of my existence. I don't think we can wait until I am older to create an army. I wish to make the area outside this village my base. My request is that you would grant me the privilege of your support."

The Elders' eyes widened, and they began to discuss amongst themselves. Several minutes later, they returned their attention to us.

Enmah answered him. "Because we are the leaders of this village, we cannot support you. That being said, we won't stop you. We will need to make an announcement tomorrow informing people that you are here and will remain close by. Having you so close could put their lives in danger, and we want to make sure they know the risk by remaining in this village. This is all we can do for you."

Greyson nodded his head in understanding.

"We would also like to speak to the king's heir in private." Drithro demanded.

The remaining four of us were promptly shooed from the tent. I walked out and pouted. I should have fought to stay. I was about to complain to Kalvin, but his gentle hand grabbed onto my arm and pulled me away from Noah and Keira.

He walked around a house into a little alley. Kalvin let go of my arm and took a deep breath. "Okay. So, before everything turns upside down, and we start risking our lives for the stupid king's heir, I need ya to know somethin'."

He looked at me with soft eyes, and I felt the sincerity in them.

I stayed quiet.

"I don't want ya to just ignore what ya heard Keira say the other night. At the time, I appreciated ya doing that. But things have changed. I don't like ya thinkin' I flirt with every girl that comes along." Kalvin smiled and took both of my hands. "Like I said before, I really only see *you*. That was the truth." Kalvin spoke as though he was going to run out of air.

He continued before I could speak.

"I'm not done. I've had feelings for ya for as long as I can remember, and I can't get over the fact that the stupid prince is comin' in and trying to steal ya away from me. So, you know what."

He took a step towards me and snaked his arm around my waist, pulling me into him.

There was a moment where he stopped moving less than a centimeter before his lips touched mine. I felt my body move forward, and our lips collided before I could process what was happening.

Passion and intensity sparked between us.

My arms found their way to rest on his upper chest, and his grip tightened around me. Both of our pulses raced.

I ran out of air and had to pull back.

There was silence between us as he held me, looking in my eyes, searching.

I barely whispered, "Kalvin..."

It snapped him out of whatever trance he was in as he let go of me and took a step back. "I'm sorry. I don't want to overwhelm ya or complicate things, and I won't do that again. I just needed ya to know all of it."

Kalvin shrugged his shoulders and smirked at me.

My immediate reaction was to punch him in the chest. As usual, he acted like it hurt him, even though it didn't.

I giggled. "You're a dork."

"I'll take it as a good sign that ya didn't run away from me," he said, then dramatically fell over, as though I really did damage to him.

We were both laughing by the time Greyson and Noah walked to us. Greyson gave me a look that I didn't understand as I collected myself and asked what the Elders said.

"It wasn't anything too important. It was just a long warning about the fact that I need to be careful who I trust from now on. The one with the blue skin said that you two should also be my closest allies."

I felt a spring of guilt in the pit of my stomach, but I tried to ignore it.

Kalvin broke the silence. "That's because my father taught me everything he knew." He turned to me, and I showed him the best smile I could muster. "And Elisia can really put battle plans together like no other. She's a clever one."

Noah looked around. "Where's Keira?"

Greyson pointed back at the tent. "She wanted to talk to the Elders about possibly staying in the village."

I spoke up afterwards before I decided to back out of my plan.

"Do you guys wanna walk me home?" I asked.

Everyone looked at me with wide eyes.

Kalvin was the first one to speak. "Are ya sure ya want to go back there? Erlan knows you're working with Greyson, and he seemed like he was going to lock ya away for not listening to him."

Greyson chimed in before I could speak. "As much as I hate to agree with him, Kalvin's right. You should stay in the village, away from your parents' house."

I held up my hand and decided on how much I was going to tell them. "I kind of have to. My mom is probably freaking out because of how long we've been gone. I also don't know how much my dad has told her about what happened. I have to go back to make sure she understands. If the end result is that I stay in the village, then I will have to pack up some more clothes and stuff to come back tomorrow." It felt wrong to lie to them, but I knew it had to be done.

Kalvin tilted his head and studied me but didn't say anything. Noah was the first to speak. "Well, whatever happens we should start heading home. I have no idea how my parents are reacting. I haven't had my phone on in days."

Greyson nodded in agreement. "We should take Elisia back first." He gave my arm a gentle squeeze. "I'm not letting you go back alone."

I gave him a small smile that was already laced with guilt.

There was a lot of confusion on the day that King Lawrence was killed. The assassins attacked on the night of September 21, 1915, the awful deed committed by the morning of September 22.

The monsters knew they needed someone to replace the king; otherwise, the human treaty would be broken. The assassins established leadership over Perfidious within the year and cobbled together a Council of five purebloods along with new high-ranking generals and court officials.

Rumors spread about Queen Miranda escaping with her unborn child on the night of the attack. Half-breeds hoped that the new Council wouldn't deter from King Lawrence's policies but soon realized how foolish that was.

Half-breeds started to die by the dozens within the mountains, and the Council of purebloods did nothing to stop it. The old Guard was disbanded, but most of their numbers remained loyal to King Lawrence and continued to look for his lost heir.

By 1997, the Council destroyed the rest of the secret camps the Guard had established in order to train new members. All rumors eventually ceased about the king's heir. However, many still believed that the widowed queen had survived and wished the heir would one day reclaim the throne, reinstating peace in Perfidious.

An excerpt from The King's Legacy:
A Complete History of Perfidious

32

We walked through the trees in silence. I waited until we were within Kalvin's hearing distance of my house. I stopped walking and turned to him.

"Can you hear if my father is home?"

I looked around the ground as Kalvin listened. Thanks to Lexon, I knew what yarrow looked like. It was everywhere. I spotted some behind me and casually grabbed a bunch of little white flowers, clutching as much as I could in my fist to keep it hidden. Kalvin had a tight expression on his face. He definitely didn't want me going in there.

"Yeah, he's home. He's talking to your mom."

I nodded and continued walking. Right before the tree line in my backyard, I turned my head to Greyson.

Searching for reassurance, I asked him, "Do you trust me?"

Greyson responded without hesitation. "With my life."

"I'd never betray that trust. Remember that," I said as I took a deep breath and steadied myself before exiting the forest.

Once I was well into the clearing of my backyard. I turned around and raised my voice loud enough for my father to hear. "Greyson, just leave me alone!"

All three of them stopped in their tracks as they looked at me. Greyson slowly shook his head. "What are you—"

"I said leave me alone! I want nothing to do with your stupid plan to help Perfidious." I took a few steps to my house.

The stubborn boy took one step towards me. "What's this about?"

"I almost died this morning because of you! Just stay away from me!" I heard the back door open. "My dad was right. I shouldn't have gotten mixed up in all of this. I should have just listened to him."

Kalvin almost looked angry. "Elisia!"

I looked Greyson straight in the eyes. "Did you even hear what I just told you?" I saw realization flicker over his features. "Leave me alone!" I yelled again as I ran inside, past my father.

I saw my mom's worried eyes, but it was my father who spoke. "Elisia?"

I turned around to look out the back door. Greyson was dragging the other two away. He looked back once before disappearing into the forest. Then I turned to face my father.

He looked at me with disbelief. His words were demanding and harsh. "What was that all about? Where have you been?"

I stared at him dead in the eyes. "You were right. I made a mistake. I want nothing to do with the humans or stupid Greyson. I want to take on my responsibility as your daughter and work with you in the castle."

Then, I prayed the yarrow worked.

ACKNOWLEDGMENTS

I want to thank my mom for making time to help me make sure everything was in order. I couldn't have gotten this far without her. I also want to thank my best friend, Annie, for lending an ear when the storyline wasn't going the way I wanted to. She really helped me calm down and think of details from a different point of view.

I also want to thank all of my editors. They didn't just help me with my manuscript, but also helped me learn more about self-publishing and gave me the confidence that it wasn't as scary as it may seem.

- P.T. McKenzie

Made in the USA
Columbia, SC
04 August 2021

42939829R00176